The Five Fathers of Pepi

THE FIVE FATHERS OF PEPI

by

IRA AVERY

THE BOBBS-MERRILL COMPANY, INC.

Indianapolis —— New York

Finale Ligure

IT IS customary to state that the characters in a work of fiction are entirely fictitious and bear no relations to living people. Such is, of course, the case with this book. But Jane and I like to think that if there *were* such people as these, they would be happiest in Finale Ligure.

IRA AVERY

Contents

The Five Fathers of Pepi

Chapter one

Giorgio

Who is there who can say with any
degree of accuracy what is likely to be going through
the head of a boy of six? Especially on a day all copper
and gold and bronze in the Italian sun, when there are
so many things to think.

Giorgio, for instance, who was thirty and consequently
did his thinking three feet farther away from the ground
than Pepi, pondered the nature of things, and the
beauty of things, and the price of things. The nature of
the railroad, whose distant gleaming tracks cut cleanly
through the white and yellow town and disappeared into
the mouth of the Varigotti tunnel. The beauty of the sea,
glinting and burnished like hammered armor plate. And
the prices that would be collected on such a splendid day

by one so fortunate as to operate Finale Ligure's finest cabana colony.

They had stopped at the top of the path, Giorgio with his hand on Pepi's shoulder. It was a silent daily ritual, a recognition that the adventure of each day started at this point on the hill, where the town first came fully into view. Giorgio's own small house was of course behind them, nestled in a hollow of the steep slope. Directly below, other houses clung precariously to the hillside, and the narrow path plunged among them with breath-taking steep turns.

Since they were above the western end of the town, most of Finale Ligure stretched away to their left, toward where the mass of Crena Point shimmered in a light haze. Nearer at hand on their right was the sheer, gaunt rock of Caprazoppa, forming the other end of a kind of giant cradle, accessible only by sea or by the twin tunnels for highway and railroad, since behind stood the Appenine barrier.

To Giorgio, and consequently to Pepi, there were four distinct levels in the town. Farthest away, lapped by the placid Gulf, was the long, narrow, gently sloping beach with its rows of cabinos and an occasional proud bath establishment. Then came the shore-front highway and the parallel Via Lido al Mare, sparsely shaded with palms and dominated at one end by Finale Ligure's sea-

14

plane factory and at the other by the square bulk of the Hotel. The third level comprised the steep alleys of the upper town, and last were the tiny farms and orchards and olive groves perched on shelves carved into the mountainside.

Giorgio found the aspect so agreeable and his thoughts so pleasant that he stood silent longer than usual. Pepi, with a native respect for the value of quiet meditation, waited dutifully.

"It is a day for thinking," said Giorgio.

Pepi nodded.

"My grandfather," said Giorgio further, "used to say that the most important thoughts of all are those with which one begins the day."

Thus prompted, Pepi surveyed the town and the beach gravely. Groves, rooftops, the early-morning traffic gliding through the tunnel, the soaring tower of the Basilica, and nearer at hand on the hillside a humbler church and a churchyard in which a figure in a tucked-up cassock was transplanting a chestnut sapling. Pepi wrinkled his brow and *thought*.

"Why is it," he said finally, "that people smell different?"

"Smell different!" echoed Giorgio in dismay.

Pepi bobbed his head emphatically. "Jacopo always smells of cheese," he declared.

15

"Naturally! He is a cheese maker."

"Benozzo smells of cigars and wine."

"True. He smells of wine because his restaurant does, and he smells of cigars because he smokes as many as he sells."

"And Carlo smells of cleaning stuff."

"Why shouldn't he? He is a Hotel porter, and the Hotel wants him to smell that way."

"Why?"

"Because," Giorgio explained patiently, "it is good business. And it is cheaper than cleaning the whole Hotel."

"Oh," said Pepi, and he bounded down the path.

Rather, he bounded in the *direction* of the path. Giorgio, following, marveled at how a six-year-old could traverse a well-worn path without ever actually setting foot on the path itself, clambering over the scuttling stones on the one side, leaping to the shade of a low-hanging peach tree on the other side. A peach tree with one plump, impudent peach hanging just at small-boy height.

"Pepi!" Giorgio shouted in warning.

Pepi paused in instant innocence, as though there were not a peach within sixty chilometri.

"Didn't you have enough breakfast?"

Pepi's eyes widened. Did anyone ever have enough breakfast?

"Besides," Giorgio added practically, "Father Luigi is watching from the churchyard."

There are times, however, when a man's reason and instinct are refuted by that department of providence which manages the affairs of small boys. Whether it was a miracle brought about because of the distant presence of Father Luigi, or whether it was because of nature's bountiful mood on such a morning, the peach chose that precise moment to plummet to the earth. In either case, Giorgio was not one to argue with the signs; he leaned over and picked up the peach.

"What do I smell like?" he asked as he handed it to Pepi.

Pepi took a large bite, considered and climbed to the top of the low stone wall that skirted the path.

"Peaches!" he sang as he hopped from stone to stone.

Of course Giorgio didn't smell in the least like a peach but saw no reason for pursuing the subject. If anything, he smelled like salt water in the summertime and dust in the winter, as befitted a man who operated a cabana colony during Finale Ligure's prosperous months and worked in the iron mines in the cold season.

Finale Ligure is what its inhabitants call a summer town. Once sturdy sailing craft from near-by Genoa and far-off Portugal, and even stealthy, arrow-breasted pirate ships symbolized the town's independence as a port, and Roman legions strode along the Via Aurelia.

17

Now its independence is mellowed with profitable hospitality, and the Via Aurelia is trod by fishermen and turisti.

Its old castle still stands, and there are even some who say that the ghost of the old Duke strides the battlements on wedding nights, complaining to the winds that things are not as they used to be when tradition accorded him the first privileges of each bridal night. Except, of course, in the case of Giorgio's own ancestress, who, according to legend, was a great beauty, yet presented herself at the castle in such an ingeniously contrived state of unattractiveness that the disheartened Duke prolonged dinner and wine until he fell into a stupor, during which she slipped away and returned to the village and her bridegroom. It is further told that when he saw her on the street some months later in her true appearance, he never drank another drop. Which, obviously, resulted in his early death. During the subsequent unprecedented surge of weddings the new Duke, who preferred falconry anyway, became hopelessly confused and actually married someone himself, a virago who forced him to abandon tradition and, ultimately, his sanity.

Finale Ligure has since, by a sort of perverse fitness, become a favorite with honeymooners and enjoys an unpretentious resort status.

Not, to be sure, the equal of San Remo and Alassio, whose beds and beaches boast a less gravelly nature, but quite satisfying to such Ligurians and Emilians as prefer spirit in their beaches and a challenge in their beds.

As to geography, Finale occupies one of the innumerable little coastwise hammocks on the western Riviera of Italy, and is a sloping half-moon of a town calling its own a small, scythelike arc of the Gulf of Savona.

It was down the most precipitous of the many mountain paths that Pepi and Giorgio came on the tawny morning, over vestigial dirt steps beaten shapeless by bare feet and goats' hoofs, past the churchyard where Father Luigi wrestled with his chestnut sapling.

"Good morning," called the priest, waving his trowel.

"Good morning," they chorused.

"It *is* a good morning," Pepi added. "There will be many customers."

"For me or for Giorgio?" asked Father Luigi.

Pepi ducked his head and dug his bare toe into the dirt. "Maybe—there will be enough to go around," he said bashfully.

Father Luigi checked Giorgio's protest with a roar of laughter, under cover of which Pepi fled the rest of the way down the path.

Giorgio wrinkled his brow in embarrassment. "Pepi . . . doesn't always say the right thing."

It was generally agreed that of all Father Luigi's accomplishments there were three things he did to angelic perfection. One was to intone a Mass, another was to make a tree grow in a place that would amaze even the tree, and the third was to take the wrinkles out of a man's brow with a smile. He smiled now, first at Pepi, waiting far down at the end of the path, and then at Giorgio.

"It isn't a bad thing," he said, "when a boy's heart is quicker than his mind. Or a man's either, for that matter."

There was something else Father Luigi did well, and that was to express a thing in such a way that you found yourself wondering later whether he meant something more than he said. Giorgio had the disconcerting feeling that the subject had been changed without his knowing it.

"The heart," Father Luigi continued, looking speculatively at his trowel as if the notes of a text were on it, "will often attempt feats that the mind would reject. Like trying to be both a father and a mother at the same time. Such a desire is admirable. The heart is often right."

From experience, Giorgio waited expectantly for a "but."

"But," said Father Luigi, turning a piece of earth with his trowel, "Pepi will be old enough for school this fall."

"Of course!" Giorgio agreed with feigned surprise. "Pepi will go to school this fall."

"Of course." Father Luigi nodded, as though completely satisfied. He pointed his chin sideways at the sapling. "The trick with a young tree, you know, is to fix it so that the roots are secure. I hope your business is good today."

"Thank you," said Giorgio, and as he walked down the hill he thought, What a wonderful advantage it is to have a priest who can think of school and a chestnut sapling and the cabana business all at the same time!

For Giorgio, Pepi's schooling was suddenly quite enough to fill his mind. It was one thing to teach a boy to swim and mind the towel lockers and count the bathhouse keys and to box his ears when he swore, but it would be another thing altogether to spend a long day in the iron mine wondering whether the boy had gone to school as he should or had chosen to pass the day looking for crickets or playing pirate in the old Neri section.

He fell into step beside Pepi, and they trudged the rest of the way into town in silence, Pepi matching each step to Giorgio's stride and taking a hop-skip every now and then to keep up. The buildings were no longer white and yellow as they had seemed from the top of the hill. They were crusty gray and dingy, with a drabness unrelieved even by their ocher blinds tightly bolted against the oncoming heat. Even the corner houses, with windowless sides painted to simulate rows of elegant casements, were a sandy monochrome of unseeing panes.

"It's going to be hot," said Pepi breathlessly, doing a double hop-skip as Giorgio's stride lengthened.

"Maybe you're not really six!" Giorgio said suddenly.

"I'm not?"

"After all, we don't *know*."

"No," said Pepi doubtfully. "But I *feel* like six."

"That," Giorgio replied scornfully, "is because I told you last year you were five."

"Wasn't I?"

"Benozzo said you were five. But who is Benozzo!"

"Vittore said I was five," Pepi ventured timidly.

Giorgio sighed. This was too true and served the purpose of making Pepi's age an unshakable fact. Where other men dealt in opinions, Vittore dealt in conclusions; his logic was unassailable, his wisdom was unchallenged. If Vittore said Pepi was five, he was the very embodiment of fiveness, as five as any boy could be. Which would now make him six. What had presented a hope of complexity was, after all, a simple, inescapable fact. There were no two ways about a conclusion of Vittore's, unless Vittore *said* there were two ways.

"It is a day for thinking," said Giorgio.

"You said that," Pepi reminded in the polite tone he reserved for impoliteness.

Giorgio ignored him. He was thinking back to the day Vittore had made his pronouncement. It was almost exactly a year ago, the day Pepi had descended on Finale Ligure. "Descended" was quite literal, for Giorgio was

going downhill from his house into the town and discovered rather abruptly that he was not alone. At first
he felt only an odd sensation of being watched, then as
he stopped halfway down the path to examine the sensation he heard soft, bare footsteps come to a stop behind
him. He turned and saw a strange, brown, ragged, large-
eyed little boy looking at him uncertainly. If Giorgio
had frowned at that moment, or suddenly rubbed his
head or scratched his arm, it's perfectly possible that
there would have been nothing but a slither of stones to
show where the little boy had stood. But, as it happened,
he smiled. At which the little boy promptly came to him
and took his hand.

In Finale Ligure no one reaches even the problemat-
ical age of five without being known from one end of the
tiny town to the other. Certain types of materializations
have been known—one is attested by a suitable shrine on
the rock shoulder of Caprazoppa—but the nonephemeral
sight of a very palpable and very dirty little boy, clinging to Giorgio's finger with a realistic grip, was hardly
such a phenomenon.

There had been no need for Giorgio to seek opinions.
They came to him unsought as the boy stood trustfully
in the center of Benozzo's restaurant, submitting to a
scrutiny by Giorgio's closest friends.

"A mountain sprite," said Benozzo.

"A mountain sprite indeed," Jacopo agreed, beaming.

"Since Carlo is busy at the Hotel and cannot be here," Benozzo volunteered, "I shall also contribute a judgment on his behalf. Being a practical man and something of a skeptic, Carlo would say, 'A runaway.' "

"A mountain sprite or a runaway," said Jacopo emphatically.

"Nonsense." Vittore snorted. "He is an orphan who has wandered over the mountains from the Po Valley."

Since investigation brought no result, Vittore's decree was, as always, accepted. And since the boy showed no indication of letting himself out of Giorgio's sight, it was decided in solemn council that Giorgio, with the moral support of the others, should stand temporarily *in loco parentis* until further disposition of the problem. It was further agreed that the boy should be called Pepi, for no reason except that the name made him smile, whereas Giovanni, Silvio, Francesco and Pietro did not.

It was established by Vittore, on the basis of size, condition of teeth, general conformation and appetite, that the boy was five. Benozzo agreed, not so much in affirmation as in desire to share the mantle of Vittore's wisdom. And Pepi was forthwith fed, scoured, clothed in what scissors and pins and Carlo's hotel-acquired dexterity with both could achieve from one of Giorgio's old shirts, and fed again.

In no time at all the boy became such a common sight, skipping along at Giorgio's side, that someone on the Via Mazzini was once heard to say, "Here come Giorgio's two shirts again!"

At which Giorgio dug into his savings and bought a uniform suitable for the small assistant of a cabana proprietor—canvas trousers and a khaki shirt exactly like his own. To this Vittore added a small silver whistle like Giorgio's, and Carlo fashioned a leather thong for it to go around the boy's neck. And Giorgio was thereafter accompanied by a diminutive copy of himself.

There was a great deal of talk, of course. The Ligurians differ from no other Italians in that their manner of speech ranges from merely loquacious to voluble. An ordinarily conversational man like Giorgio, for instance, would be considered quiet, while a quiet man like Carlo would be classed as almost suspiciously taciturn.

It was nevertheless Carlo who first said:

"The boy should be adopted by rich Americans."

Benozzo instantly endorsed the idea, and so did Jacopo. Giorgio, who prided himself on being unsentimental, shrugged. Vittore, after criticizing Carlo mildly for redundancy, announced that the motion was carried.

"Carlo will notify us when Americans arrive at the Hotel," said Vittore. "Jacopo will ingratiate himself with them and suggest Benozzo's restaurant as an ideal eating place—for which he will say three Hail Marys—and Giorgio will deliver Pepi upon my signal."

So it was that Pepi was scrubbed and trotted out on at least three occasions before American turisti who found him extremely appealing but who proved blankly impervious to innuendo. So Pepi had spent the rest of the summer at the cabana and the ensuing winter playing in the iron mine or exploring the hills.

Now it was summer again, and the topic had not been brought up. Or if it had, Giorgio seemed always to have chosen just that moment to engage Benozzo in an argument or to pose a point of logic to Vittore or to remark on an expensive passing car. It may, of course, have been nothing but coincidence, even when he attempted all three things at once.

"A conversation is difficult enough," Benozzo had once observed a little pettishly, "when it is disarranged by five single trains of thought. But when one of these new talkative moods strikes Giorgio, he is like a man riding all ten horses in the Palio."

Jacopo nodded.

"He is in love," Carlo suggested.

"Of course he is in love," Vittore declared. "All young men are in love."

Since Giorgio's opinion was not asked, he was happily able to keep quiet.

As a matter of fact, while he was not actually in love, or at least had not taken the time to decide officially whether he was or not, most of Finale Ligure had speculated on this topic, too. Giorgio's means, by local standards, were not inconsiderable, consisting as they did of a modest "marriage fund," arbitrarily so-called in the case of a bachelor, and the small, solid house on the hill. He was employed in both winter and summer, which was a rarity. He was handsome, which was an asset. And he was sincerely unaware of his handsomeness, which was a blessing. In short, he was a prize.

The other side of the equation, as seen by the townsfolk, was the olivegrower Giulio Bonelli's eldest daughter, Maria, who had all the things a girl should have, and spirit besides. The fact that Giorgio and Maria had attended the Carnevale together after Pepi had gone to bed provided, to everyone but Giorgio, all the elements of a foregone conclusion. Even his four friends, who prided themselves on their hard-won bachelorhood, recognized the signs. Giorgio himself was accorded the usual privilege of being given time to arrive at the same conclusion independently.

On just such a morning as this, as Giorgio and Pepi strode (or skipped, in Pepi's case) beneath the dusty palms toward the center of town, whence they would turn toward the beach, passers-by would cluck to themselves and say, "If it weren't for Pepi . . . !"

Meanwhile Giorgio, deep in thought, clucked to himself and said, "If it weren't for school . . . !"

Everyone knows that a person chooses his own difficulties, and any bystander would have told Giorgio that he had chosen the wrong one. But the wrong difficulty often looms as large as the right one, and Giorgio, having made his choice, wrestled with Pepi's schooling.

Pepi must go to school, certainly. But why was there in that thought so much seriousness, so much of a suggestion of change from the past? Pepi had been little responsibility so far, officiating happily over the keys and towels, sleeping where and when he saw fit, eating by turns at Benozzo's restaurant, in the Hotel kitchen with Carlo, or munching a curd in Jacopo's tiny cheese factory. But school—here was the beginning of a whole new life, something to be reckoned with. Order and regimentation, letters and numbers and starched Sisters, seriousness and discipline, the beginning of manhood. This was responsibility, moral as well as financial.

"Ferrari!" yelled Pepi as a bright-red open car whirled by on the Via Aurelia.

Giorgio smiled and nodded approvingly. There was a girl in the car, and he struggled with the intrusion of a second line of thought, one which dealt with perfume and blue-black hair and a Carnevale and the spicy redolence of the olivegrower Giulio Bonelli's parlor. It was

28

just a passing thought; Giorgio was astounded at its impudence.

"Will we stop at Benozzo's to say good morning?" asked Pepi.

"Why not?"

"You look so serious. I thought you might forget."

"Serious! Nonsense!"

He cuffed the boy playfully on the head, and Pepi raced away as though set off by an invisible trigger, his bare feet pelting the hot pavement and his silver whistle jouncing on its thong over his shoulder.

Giorgio sighed and slowed his walk.

"It is a day for thinking," he said aloud for the third time.

Chapter two

Benozzo

Aɴʏ Italian town, for the sake of its own dignity, must have at least one outstanding landmark, one distinctive sight to live in the memory of travelers. In Finale Ligure this purpose was served by Benozzo's mustache.

There were other attractions, to be sure. Olive groves, pine trees, beeches—graceful and fragrant, all of them, but scarcely unique in a land of such beauties. Watchtowers, an arch, a fine church—Finale had all these, but the watchtowers and the church might as well be anywhere on the Riviera, and the Spanish Arch, dourly dominating the Piazza XXV Aprile in the middle of town, stood little chance for immortality, since Benozzo's restaurant was directly opposite.

After all, the true test of a landmark is its performance in competition, and any stranger stopping squarely in front of the Spanish Arch at a moment when Benozzo happened to appear before his restaurant could never for the rest of life recite the dimensions of the Arch with any accuracy.

It should not therefore be conluded that Benozzo's mustache won its distinction entirely by default. Its magnificence was intrinsic. To say merely that it was a large mustache would do it incomplete justice. To describe it as graceful, curly and of an admirable (if slightly suspicious) blackness would deprive it of its full due. It was a behemoth of a mustache.

Where ordinary mustaches remind one of motorcycle handle bars, Benozzo's would bring to mind the dividing of a great wave before a ship's prow. It was such a mustache that it seemed to enter a room separately, in advance of its owner. And in the manner of fasces borne before an ancient dignitary, it endowed Benozzo with an enviable authority.

It was, moreover, a *thinking* mustache. It would twitch and quiver over the selection of a wine, tremble with anticipatory laughter during the telling of a joke and virtually pulsate to its curled ends over the adding of a row of figures. While it would be unjust to say that Benozzo's own mental prowess was inferior to that of his mustache, it could scarcely be denied that he depended on it for assistance and that he treated it with

31

suitable affection. He was, after all, the custodian of a landmark.

At eight-thirty on a splendid morning like this the mustache was at its best. Benozzo thrived on Organization and Decisions, and both were brought into play at such an hour on such a day. Organization. Order. Planning. At eight-forty the bicycle of the fishmonger's boy would clatter against the corner post, and there would be fish to select. From the pavement, of course; this was the invariable result of the fishmonger's boy's poor sense of direction and inevitable collision. At eight-forty-five the bicycle of the baker's boy would upset the bicycle of the fishmonger's boy and there would be bread. Everywhere. At eight-fifty Jacopo would arrive from his cheese factory with a basket of plump, fresh balls of ricotta; at eight-fifty-five it would be time to telephone the butcher; and at nine o'clock Fortunato the vegetable vendor would rattle to a stop in his antiquity of a wagon.

All of this *would* happen, that is, on a millennial day. It would be more truthful to say that the baker's boy would arrive between eight-forty-five and eleven-thirty, that the fishmonger's boy might not arrive at all and that Jacopo and Fortunato had encountered each other on the street and were talking politics while the ricotta and the artichokes and the eggplants simmered in the sun. And the first hour of the day would be spent in deciding whether to call the butcher or polish glasses. Or in pleasant conversation with Giorgio and Pepi, who were already in sight across the Piazza.

Benozzo's mustache emerged into the sunlight from the cavernous open front of his restaurant. At which Pepi gave a small, disappointed yelp to himself; he secretly supposed the thing to be removable and had waited out the year in the excited hope that Benozzo might one morning forget to attach it. However, these are thoughts that a boy keeps to himself. He quickly turned the yelp into a cry of greeting.

Benozzo waved with a big hand that held a towel and a wineglass.

"Any time you don't need him any more," he said to Giorgio with a wink, "I'll take him. I'd rather have one of Pepi than two of that worthless Tonio!"

Tonio, who was very skinny and never seemed to know quite what to do with his bony, dangling hands and whose mouth was perpetually half open, always made Pepi think of a marionette whose strings had become tangled. He giggled at the idea of two Tonios, breaking twice as many glasses.

"Come in, come in," said Benozzo. "Sit down. When Tonio comes he will make us some coffee. Late! He is always late. No sense of responsibility!"

Benozzo consulted a huge watch and groaned in despair.

"Why does your watch *always* say two-thirty?" asked Pepi, pointing.

Benozzo shrugged. "Because that is when it stopped," he said simply. "I thought of having it fixed, but there is an old man in the Neri section who used to be a watch-maker and who advised me against it."

"Why?"

"Because one has no need to worry about whether a watch is wrong when one *knows* it is wrong. If it were running, I should be constantly wondering about it and running across the Piazza to check it against the clock in the bank, and banks depress me. They are jails for money, and money should be out in the open, doing things for people."

"But how do you know what time it is?" Pepi persisted.

Benozzo breathed on a wineglass and polished it with vigor.

"That is easy," he replied. "I know it is after seven because I am awake and in my restaurant. And I know it is after eight because you and Giorgio are here. But it is not *much* after eight or Giorgio would be hurrying faster to open the cabanas. And I'll tell you something else, Pepi," he said with a magnificent flourish of his mustache. "*My* watch has a distinction not possessed by many others. At least twice a day it is *exactly* right!"

Pepi, impressed, picked up a wineglass, breathed on

it prodigiously and began polishing it with a towel.

Benozzo looked at Giorgio with concern.

"Is something the matter, *amico?* You are too solemn. Your face is like my brother Bernardo's when his sight-seeing bus from Alassio breaks down in front of my restaurant every Thursday."

Giorgio shook his head. "Nothing is the matter," he said.

"Nothing is the matter!" repeated Benozzo scornfully to Pepi. "If it were Carlo, now, with a face that always looks like a sick horse . . . but Giorgio! Look at him!"

Pepi put down the glass and turned gravely. Giorgio squirmed and scratched his neck.

"Do you think you are hiding your feelings by saying nothing?" said Benozzo severely. "Giorgio, I am your friend!"

"I know that."

"Then you won't mind if I tell you frankly that you are not a very good actor. This is not a criticism, you understand. I don't require of my friends that they be good actors. But you might at least say, 'I have a difficulty, but I do not wish to discuss it,' instead of sitting there insisting nothing is the matter when a fly would break his leg trying to walk over the wrinkles in your forehead!"

Giorgio felt his forehead guiltily and opened his mouth.

"Oh, not that you have to *tell* me!" Benozzo pursed his lips and the mustache lifted like the wings of a gigantic raven. "That Tonio! He has only two accomplishments. Sleeping and oversleeping! I shall make the coffee myself."

He filled a machinetta pot, lighted the flame under a pan of water and selected a gnarled black cigar from a drawer under the counter, squinting at Pepi as he did so.

"Pepi."

"Yes, Benozzo?"

"Coffee draws bitterness from the brain, and a peel of lemon draws bitterness from the coffee. Please run down the street and find Fortunato's wagon. Tell him to give you a lemon on account."

Pepi looked at Giorgio.

"Go ahead," Giorgio nodded, and Pepi whirled out under the red-and-orange canopy, arousing a dozen lazy flies which buzzed irately and settled down again.

Benozzo aimed a thoughtful cloud of blue cigar smoke at the nearest fly and watched it escape drunkenly.

"As I say," he remarked, "there is no need to tell *me*. I am not a curious man. If you choose not to discuss the matter, that is an end of it. I shall not inquire further."

He lined up his glasses with elaborate care.

"But what is it!" he finally exploded.

"Benozzo," Giorgio began, chewing on his lip, "I

don't know. Is it possible to be worried about something and not know what it is?"

The mustache thought this over.

"It depends," said Benozzo finally. "If you have had a quarrel with Maria . . . yes, it is possible. Because when a woman quarrels she has a way of ending it so that you have no idea what the quarrel was about—only that you were in the wrong."

Giorgio sighed heavily and fingered a gleaming wineglass, which Benozzo gently rescued.

"No," he said. "No quarrel."

"You are perhaps—going to quarrel then?"

"No."

"Then Maria must have been struck dumb."

"Why do you say that?"

Benozzo placed the glass on the counter and leaned on both hands.

"Giorgio," he said, "I am not a wise man like our friend Vittore. But I am a clever man, and *per Bacco,* I know about people. Women like things according to the order of nature, which is number one to have enough money to marry them, number two to have enough money to buy clothes for their children, and number three to have enough money to send the children to school—this is without reckoning earrings and new dresses. Anything else is against the order of nature. You are worrying about this and so is Maria, and therefore you will have a quarrel. Probably about something else."

"Maybe I won't marry," said Giorgio unhappily.

"Nonsense!"

"You didn't marry."

Benozzo regarded him patiently. "I told you, I am a clever man." He shrugged. "We cannot all be clever, or the human race would die out.

"Don't think I'm heartless," he said as he relighted his cigar, "but orphanages are not so bad. Carlo spent his boyhood in an orphanage, and he learned to make medals."

"But Carlo doesn't make medals. He is a hotel porter."

"True. That proves there is a shortage of at least one maker of medals."

He searched under the counter for coffee cups and came up a trifle short-winded.

"Giorgio, listen to me. We are not rich men, you and I. Finale Ligure is not a town of rich men. It is, thank the Blessed Madonna, not a town of very poor men either. There is employment, but just enough for those of us who live here. And only half the year in most cases. I feed the boy, don't I?"

Giorgio nodded.

"If I could do more . . . if he smoked cigars, perhaps . . ."

The two men looked at each other, and Giorgio forced

a smile. "It's all right, Benozzo. Only I must think some more."

Benozzo poured the hot water into the machinetta pot. "Some coffee while you think?"

Giorgio shook his head slowly and walked out toward the sun-drenched Piazza.

"Don't forget," called Benozzo, "to tell me all about the quarrel!"

But though his tone was light, his eyebrows were together and his splendid mustache trembled thoughtfully.

Giorgio stepped into the Square. Under the Spanish Arch a straw-hatted cloth merchant was setting up his merchandise. A donkey-drawn wine cart clattered in the shadows of the alley. Across the Via Aurelia the cabana owners were taking down their canvas and preparing to open for business, and somewhere people were shouting. A mile out at sea a bright-blue sail strained in a stiff breeze. There was a smell of wine and mandarins and acacia, and the faint whiff of a gnarled black cigar.

Pepi was nowhere to be seen. Giorgio lifted the silver whistle on its leather thong and blew a shrill blast. He waited, and an answering note trilled from the distance.

"Giorgio!"

He turned to see Benozzo beckoning him back.

"Giorgio, I've been thinking. There are enough medal makers."

Giorgio stepped into the shade of the awning.

"In Milan," Benozzo said, "I've heard they are on every street corner, and some of them have fine shops. Who is going to set Pepi up in a fine shop?"

"I don't know."

"I am almost as much a father to Pepi as you are."

"That is true."

"Where did you bring him when you found him? To my restaurant! Where did Vittore first see Pepi?"

"In your restaurant."

"And Jacopo?"

"In your restaurant."

"And Carlo?"

"In the Hotel, when Pepi saw Carlo in the elevator and thought he was a prisoner——"

Benozzo waved impatiently. "No matter. In principle, I have more right to worry about Pepi than anyone except you."

"I remember the elevator because he wanted to take food to Carlo——"

"Will you stop talking a lot of nonsense and listen to me! What I'm trying to say is, why don't you *ask* Maria about Pepi?"

"Ask her?"

"It might be that . . . well, who knows? *Have* you asked her?"

"No. What . . . would I say?"

Benozzo scratched his head. "Well. There is this about such a conversation, especially with a girl like Maria. It depends a great deal on following the processes of a woman's mind, and of course if you could do that, no woman would have anything to do with you!"

There was a pounding of bare feet and Pepi ran up to them breathlessly. "Fortunato will be late this morning!" he announced, panting.

"Fortunato?"

Pepi produced a lemon in explanation. "He will be late," he said excitedly, "because of the bathtub."

"Bathtub!" they both exclaimed.

"The bathtub in Signor Blengino's parlor."

Giorgio and Benozzo looked at each other.

"Have you been in any trouble?" asked Giorgio suspiciously.

"Trouble, Giorgio?" Pepi's eyes were wide with innocence.

"What is this about a bathtub in Signor Blengino's parlor?"

"Oh, that. That was only because it wouldn't go through the front door."

"What?"

Pepi nodded emphatically. "It wasn't until after the window got broken in the fight that somebody noticed the window was bigger than the door, so they put the

41

bathtub through the window, only now it won't go up the stairs, so Signor Blengino is going to keep it in the parlor."

"The fight? There was a fight?"

"Oh, yes, a fine one! That was because Fortunato's horse stepped in the bathtub."

Giorgio spread his hands helplessly. "It is always like this! Such lies! Why do little boys lie?"

"But it's the truth, Giorgio! Every word!"

"You said the bathtub was in Signor Blengino's *parlor*."

"That was *afterward*. First there was the fight, because while it was in the street Fortunato's horse tried to step in it, and Signor Blengino said he would have to pay, and Fortunato said *he* would have to pay for injuring his horse—he wasn't really injured of course, only surprised——"

"Surprised? What do you mean?"

"Because of the *fight!*" said Pepi with mild exasperation. "Didn't I *tell* you?"

"Pepi—" Giorgio's voice was as stern as he could make it—"what was the fight about?"

"Well, it was . . . people throwing things."

"Did *you* throw things?"

"Maybe . . . once—" then quickly—"but only once, Giorgio. Just one tiny lemon. It was no good anyway—that's why I threw it back."

"You see?" said Giorgio anxiously to Benozzo.

"Anyway," Pepi went on plaintively, "as you can see, if it hadn't been for me, they would never have got the bathtub in."

"Wait," said Benozzo. "Let me try. Pepi."

"Yes, Benozzo?"

"What do you mean, you threw the lemon 'back'?"

Pepi sighed and traced a circle with one bare toe on the pavement. This is the way things are, the circle said: you tell a perfectly simple story and grownups get it all mixed up.

"I thought it was better not to bother Fortunato, since he was so busy trying to get his wagon around the bathtub," he explained.

"So you helped yourself to a lemon."

Pepi nodded. "Only I got two by mistake, and one wasn't very good." He looked at Giorgio imploringly. "Wasn't I right to return it?"

"You returned it," said Giorgio, "by way of the horse?"

"That . . . was an accident. I really aimed for the wagon—truly, Giorgio. It was the wind, I think."

"There is no wind, except on the water."

"Well, there must have been *some*, because the lemon went crooked. Or maybe," he said logically, "it was because the lemon was in the way of being flat on one side."

"Giorgio! Benozzo!"

43

It was pudgy little Jacopo, trotting across the Piazza and puffing. "Fortunato says he will be late this morning."

"So Pepi tells us," said Benozzo wryly.

Jacopo mopped his shining forehead with a large white handkerchief. "There was a big bathtub being moved into Blengino's," he said, "and Fortunato stopped to watch, and somebody hit the horse with a lemon——"

"Pepi!" Giorgio shouted, but Pepi was halfway across the Piazza.

"A small boy is something of a responsibility," Benozzo observed.

"Yes, indeed," agreed Jacopo, not because he understood the connection, but because it was Jacopo's nature to be agreeable.

Chapter three

Jacopo

JACOPO was, in fact, as agreeable a man as you could hope to find. Round as one of his own fat, white cheeses and as bland, his chief contribution to any conversation was to punctuate it with affirmation. The most specious assertion could draw from Jacopo as ready a beaming assent as the simplest verity.

"In any case," said Giorgio, his eyes on the vanishing figure of Pepi, who had now crossed the Square and was darting skillfully through the morning traffic on the Via Aurelia, "Pepi will do a good morning's work—if only to stay busy so I won't scold him!"

Jacopo nodded amiably and tied his large handkerchief in its accustomed place around his neck. "It is a certainty," he agreed, wondering vaguely why Pepi should have to be scolded.

"Also in any case," announced Benozzo, sniffing the lemon Pepi had left, "we shall now have our coffee with lemon peel. And," he added, "with service."

The last was inspired by the approach across the Square of the prodigal Tonio, whose habitual gait seemed less of a walk than an amazing process of folding and unfolding, which he was able to arrest at any moment in a sort of angular repose. He came to a stop before them and stood as though leaning against an unseen support.

"There was a great battle in the street," he explained, gesturing with bony fingers to imply chaos. "Good morning."

"By night," said Benozzo, "the affair of Fortunato's horse will have become an engagement equaling the siege of Sicily. Good morning."

"Or even the landing at Aspromonte!" said Jacopo. "Good morning, Tonio."

"They will probably blame those on Pepi, too," Giorgio groaned. "Good morning."

"Nonsense!" Benozzo tossed the lemon to Tonio. "You may fix us some coffee."

Tonio cradled the lemon in his large hands and stared at it as he sidled into the restaurant. It is an interesting thing, he thought, that on some days you will hear a certain unfamiliar word two or more times, and on some days four different people will order the same meal independently, and on still other days everyone seems to be throwing lemons! There could not, of course, be any mystical significance in such cycles, but on the other hand—it pays to be safe. And before he sliced the peel from the lemon he threw it into the air several times.

"There is nothing wrong with Pepi," Benozzo said, "except that he needs a mother."

"It is a good thing to have a mother," Jacopo agreed.

He reflected on the truth of this observation as they seated themselves at one of the outside tables and inhaled the whorls of steam from their coffee cups. His own mother had succeeded in protecting him, to some degree at least, from six older sisters.

There were many in Finale Ligure who said, with compassionate rather than uncharitable intent, that it was this same formidable female atmosphere, rather than a love of music, which drove Jacopo's father to become the most regular and by all odds the best-rehearsed saxhorn player in the Varigotti band. Jacopo certainly recalled many nights during his boyhood when his father had quietly left the shrill cacophony of the kitchen and had retired to the tiny cheese factory behind the house, from which there would later come reverberant cadenzas and blasting runs that made him shiver with delight.

When Jacopo later made his own escape to the sanctuary of the army, it was generally thought that he was the unlikeliest of soldiers. But, as it happened, he was a singular success. Not only did his placid, unresistant nature make him a model of discipline to his own officers and a favorite of the invading Americans, but he also won the distinction of being the infantryman who found the early-morning bugle call so stimulating that he was invariably the first to turn out.

"Perhaps," Jacopo suggested, "Pepi should learn to play a musical instrument."

"Musical instruments cost money," said Benozzo.

"Besides," said Giorgio, puzzled, "what has a musical instrument got to do with having a mother?"

"A mother?" Jacopo sighed. Sometimes it was impossible to follow the processes of Giorgio's mind.

Benozzo gingerly extracted the piece of lemon peel from his coffee and sucked it thoughtfully. "*Everything* costs money," he observed.

"Cheese," Jacopo ventured modestly, "is still something of a bargain." He turned to Giorgio.

"My father's old saxhorn still hangs on its peg in the back of the cheese factory," he said. "It is a formidable instrument for so small a boy, but——"

"No, thank you," said Giorgio quickly. "I have enough problems already." Then, seeing Jacopo's crestfallen look, he added with a smile, "Besides—you musn't give Pepi any more presents. It was you who gave him his goat."

Jacopo, somewhat mollified, untied his neckerchief and mopped his brow.

"It was nothing," he said. "A boy needs the companionship of an animal. One can learn much from goats. Patience. Philosophy."

Benozzo put the flat of one hand on the tiny table and stroked his mustache with the other.

"This is not solving the problem in hand," he said sternly. "One can learn patience and philosophy from . . . from a cigar."

"You are perfectly right," Jacopo nodded. "However, there is this to be said. A cigar does not have the loyalty of a goat. It will allow itself to be smoked by anyone."

"A cigar also does not have the appetite of a goat." Benozzo dismissed the subject with a wave of his hand. "There is no argument."

Giorgio looked from one to the other in wonderment. "What is this about cigars and goats?"

Then Jacopo remembered. "What is the problem in hand?" he asked.

"Pepi," said Benozzo ponderously.

"What has he done?"

"He has done nothing except to become six years old. He should have a mother to see that he is dressed properly and goes to school every day."

"School," Giorgio suggested hopefully, "does not begin until fall."

"But a problem must be faced and solved. It is the only way."

"It is the only way," Jacopo agreed. "That is—if there is a solution."

"There is always a solution of some kind."

Giorgio shook his head. "There are solutions to be talked about," he corrected, "and solutions to be done. Sometimes they are not the same."

"That is very true," said Jacopo, nodding more vigorously than ever. "I observed it to be so in the army."

"Military science is another thing altogether," said Benozzo patiently. "It is divided into two classes of operation—the planning and the action. If they were identical, what would be the need of both?"

Giorgio stood up. "I am going to work," he announced. "Pepi is not allowed to drink soft drinks in the morning, and—well, he sometimes forgets."

"I'll walk with you," said Jacopo. "Thank you for the coffee, Benozzo."

"Tonio!" Benozzo bellowed, waving for the cups to be removed. "I would walk with you too, but a man in the restaurant business has no leisure. There is much to do."

As if on signal, the baker's boy limped into view on a

bicycle almost as uncertain as its rider. Benozzo's shout so unnerved him that he abruptly backpedaled at the exact moment a coughing Fiat was negotiating the turn beside the Arch, with results both instantaneous and novel.

As luck would have it, the driver of the Fiat was already purple with frustration at the normal traffic. To him the tooth-jarring impact was another in a succession of indignities, but the sight of the terrified baker's boy sitting astride his car bonnet, clutching a single salvaged loaf to his breast—this was a crowning insult! He scrambled out of the car and began screaming what seemed to be amounts of money—a catalogue, it soon developed, of repair costs, including an estimate for a fender of seasoned looseness.

"Genoese!" Benozzo snorted, his patriotism afire, and he strode into the melee, with Giorgio and Jacopo at his heels.

With the help of numerous bystanders and a white-helmeted policeman, who had been sucking a lemon in the shadow of the Arch, the driver was ultimately persuaded to settle for two loaves of bread and drove off with appropriate mechanical sputters. The baker's boy, save for certain minor bruises which he considered too delicate for discussion, was more damaged from examination than from the accident; and as for the bicycle, its performance was, if anything, slightly improved by the experience.

Except for several well-trampled loaves of bread, the only real casualty was Tonio, whose reaction on seeing the policeman's half-finished lemon hurtling through the air was to retreat behind the counter more rapidly than gracefully, skinning both knuckles. Twice later he was seen to shake his head and mutter cryptically, "The Day of the Lemons!"

Leaving the Square, where eyewitnesses to the mishap had now tripled and were in high-pitched conflict, Giorgio and Jacopo turned into the bicycle lane that ran between the highway and the Via Lido. Here a layer of fine sand whispered under their feet and whirled in little eddies as cars zoomed by. The gay canopies of the cabana row fluttered halfheartedly in a desultory breeze. Jacopo, who had almost as much trouble as Pepi matching Giorgio's strides, scurried to keep pace. "I have a problem too, Giorgio," he said, measuring breathlessly the distance to the blue-and-gold awning of Giorgio's establishment. "Perhaps you can advise me."

Giorgio shrugged. "I am a poor one for advice, Jacopo. However . . ."

"How can one learn to speak English very quickly?"

"How much English?"

"Oh, very much. Enough to carry on a conversation."

Giorgio stopped and scratched his head. "I don't know. There are books."

"Did you learn from books?"

"From books and from my father, before he died. He made me learn German, too. My father was not a man to take chances."

"They are not fast enough. If *you* could teach me . . . only you are too busy."

"Why must you learn to speak English in such a hurry?"

"I'll tell you. Only—*how* can I learn?"

"Well." Giorgio considered. "One should learn to speak a language from a scholar, and the only scholar we know is Vittore."

Jacopo sighed. "Vittore is a perfectionist. Vittore would say I do not even speak Italian well enough to learn another language."

"There are records that one can play on a machine."

"Yes," said Jacopo ruefully. "I bought one and played it on my sister Josefina's machine. It says, 'I am standing,' and 'I am sitting,' and 'The color of the ceiling is blue.' But these things one can see for oneself. I can now say, 'This is a box. There is a pencil in the box.' But what can one do if there is neither a pencil nor a box to talk about?"

"If you would tell me why it is so necessary to learn

to speak English . . . French would be much easier."

"It is necessary because I am expecting visitors, and they speak no Italian."

"English visitors?"

"No. American."

"Oh." Giorgio frowned. "That is a very difficult kind of English. You must know the names of baseball teams."

"You see—" Jacopo struggled with his trouser pocket and extracted a wrinkled letter—"there was a soldier in the American army—we became very good friends, but that was because he spoke Italian. And now a friend of his is coming here on his vacation."

He offered the letter to Giorgio.

DEAR JACOPO,

An old friend of mine, Harry Clune, and his wife are spending their vacation in Europe this summer and will be driving from Paris to Rome some time in July. I told them to be sure to stop in Finale Ligure and meet you.

They had what we call in America a "tough break" last winter—maybe you can get somebody to translate that for you, I can't say it in Italian—and this vacation is very important to them. I told them you would show them real old-fashioned Italian hospitality.

Harry is a very important man in the automobile business in New York. You will like his wife. They both like good food, but they don't speak Italian, so they will appreciate having a friend.

If you are ever in New York, you have my address. It is not much compared to Harry's house in Connecticut, but it is near a good Italian restaurant on 56th Street where they serve spaghetti with real Genoese pesto.

Take care of Harry and Betty for me. And come to New York soon.

A rivederci,
JIM

"So," said Jacopo, "I must learn to speak English very quickly. What is a 'tough break'?"

Giorgio wrinkled his forehead. "In America a 'tough break' is to lose a bet on a baseball game. Everything is baseball."

"How can I learn about baseball?" Jacopo mourned. "I cannot even understand cricket."

One of the great mysteries in Jacopo's life had been an exhibition cricket match played in Finale the month before. He mistook the first two hours of play for an unconscionably long warm-up and assumed the match to be over at the end of the first day. And worse, he had allowed Benozzo to shout him into endless bets which ultimately amounted to five million lire. The actual payment of the bet had been two bottles of Orvieto, but the unnerved cricketers had left Finale convinced that fortunes had changed hands.

"How does one entertain Americans?" asked Jacopo forlornly.

Giorgio spread his hands.

"It is not necessary to entertain Americans. They entertain themselves. If they like to swim, they may have the best cabana on my beach. Carlo will see that they have a good room at the Hotel, and Benozzo will feed them."

"And the language? Will you help me, Giorgio?"

"It is already July! How can I teach you English in no time at all?"

Bathers were laughing and shouting on the beach, and Giorgio looked anxiously toward his cabanas, still a hundred meters distant.

"Then you will talk to them? And signal me when to say 'yes' and 'no'?" Jacopo's eyes were beseeching.

Giorgio laughed. "All right. I will talk to them."

"Who knows?" said Jacopo as they started walking again. "Perhaps this will be the solution to your problem, too!"

"My problem?"

"Of Pepi, of course. If the Americans have no children . . ."

But the roar of a passing car drowned Giorgio's reply. Jacopo looked up at him and decided in view of Giorgio's grimly set jaw, which betokened sudden preoccupation, that he would not repeat. Cricket matches, Benozzo's logic and Giorgio's abrupt moods of late were phenomena which belonged, Jacopo sadly reflected, to a rarefied stratum accessible only to intellects greater than his.

He brightened as he saw Carlo approaching. Here was a man who, although an unremitting cynic, was at least comprehensible.

Chapter four

Carlo

WHILE the little open-fronted res-
taurant on the Square was to Benozzo's own friends the
official clearinghouse of all local news and opinion, it was
by no means the only such place in Finale Ligure. In
fact, every other restaurant as well as the railroad station, the post office, the cinema lobby and the town hall
held the same status. Where one finally verified or
otherwise disposed of information was a matter of personal loyalty, so that it was perfectly possible for a
dozen different versions of a given event to become
equally official and pass into a history confusing only
to an outsider.

However, in the two hours immediately preceding the
noonday meal and the two hours following the same

meal, all partisans withdrew to the broad, canopied cabana verandas, driven in by the heat of the town on the one side and the heat of the beach on the other. These were interludes reserved for the discussion of politics, business, sports, world affairs and other topics of the larger and vaguer order.

In this scheme of things the position of the Hotel was unique: it served as a definite link with the outer world, an unimpeachable source of plain facts. There could be no two opinions about the fact that the occupant of Room 207 was an archaeologist en route to Siena, or that the French lady in Room 415 was not the wife of the French gentleman in Room 415, or that the American schoolteachers in Room 301 diluted their vino rosso with San Bernardo water and thought Italian policemen were the handsomest men in the world.

The simplicity and truth of such facts were the badge of an emissary who never used two words where one would suffice. Long before Carlo had become senior porter at the Hotel he had developed a reportorial accuracy, not for its own sake, but because he found it saved him words. This economy, along with a naturally sad demeanor and an extravagant length of face, served him well at both ends of his calling. On the one hand, guests at the Hotel would glance at him only to reassure themselves that the elevator was safe and proceed to discuss their affairs freely. And on the other hand, his friends accorded him an honored place as one who surely must know more than he was saying.

His walk alone would easily have identified him as either a hotel porter or a professional mourner. Even the slight stoop deceived many sympathetic strangers who attributed it to the weight of grief rather than suitcases.

He smiled, if it can be said that an almost imperceptible parting of the lips is a smile, when he saw Giorgio and Jacopo and, seeing that the encounter was inevitable, preserved his energy by stopping and waiting.

"Good morning," he said. "Jacopo, the manager asked me to find you."

He dug into the porter's apron rolled about his middle and drew out a letter.

Jacopo seized it eagerly and then looked at Giorgio with dismay. "It's in English!" he exclaimed.

Giorgio took it from him and frowned over it.

"It is your friends," he said finally. "They have reserved a room for next week—Tuesday—and they ask the Hotel to let you know they are coming."

"Yes," said Carlo, nodding lugubriously.

"Giorgio! Carlo! What shall I do?"

"We shall talk about it," Giorgio promised. "Now I must go. If Pepi gets bored, he will tell somebody he sees a shark, just for excitement."

"But there are no sharks!"

"*I* know that, and Pepi knows it. But if he says he sees one, six customers will see it too."

"Giorgio," Jacopo called after him. "Does the letter say if they have children?"

Giorgio stopped without turning around. "No," he said. "But it doesn't say they do *not* have children either."

And he continued walking toward the cabanas, but more slowly.

"Children?" Carlo repeated, raising one eyebrow a fraction.

Jacopo nodded. "Benozzo thinks we should try again to have Pepi adopted."

Carlo considered. "What does Giorgio think?"

Jacopo untied his handkerchief and mopped his forehead.

"Giorgio?" he sighed. "Who knows what Giorgio thinks! Every time one tries to talk to him, he is busy in his mind about something."

"Perhaps," Carlo suggested, "he wants us to decide for him."

Jacopo looked at him anxiously. "Should we?"

"Let me see the letter."

He studied it slowly. "It comes from a very good hotel in Paris. That means they are wealthy."

"I . . . I don't know. Maybe we should see what Vittore thinks."

"Vittore is on the beach in front of Giorgio's cabanas," said Carlo. "I could see him from the Hotel."

Jacopo's relief was immediate and apparent. "Then we can't possibly talk to him. Giorgio would see us. Besides, I must deliver my cheeses."

They parted, Jacopo hesitantly choosing a place to cross the highway where two arguing flower sellers had slowed traffic to a standstill, Carlo plodding back along the bicycle path toward the end of town dominated by the Hotel's six-story splendor.

He stopped for a moment before the tentlike entrance that bore the small, proud placard:

CAPPELLETTI GIORGIO
PROPR.

On the veranda leading to the beach Giorgio was busily stacking towels behind the counter and checking off the list of occupied bathhouses as Pepi recited them loudly and authoritatively. Carlo, schooled in noticing details, observed that someone had just presented Pepi with a bottle of raspberry soda in defiance of morning rules.

He walked on, deep in thought.

Carlo's own share in the responsibility for Pepi had come rather late. He was, in fact, not particularly fond of small boys, whom he found to be almost universally troublesome in hotels and an absolute menace in elevators. True, it might be said he had served as the boy's tailor, but it was not until Pepi had been among them for over a month that he had been pressed into additional service.

It was on a day when one of the turisti had left a valuable package at the Hotel by mistake and telephoned in consternation from Genoa mere hours before sailing. Carlo had been chosen to deliver the package in person to the pier, an event which warranted his being conducted to the railroad station by all his friends. Benozzo had contributed a bottle of Chianti for the journey, and the others vied in offering advice on travel deportment.

Giorgio was the one who had first noticed Pepi's vast excitement. "You'd think—" he laughed—"that he was going himself!"

There was a stir as an identical thought occurred to Benozzo and Vittore.

"It's only half fare," Benozzo remarked.

"He'd be company for Carlo," Vittore added.

And, following a hurried scramble for money, Carlo found himself on the train with a small companion.

At that, it seemed as though it wouldn't be so much trouble as he'd thought. The compartment was not crowded, and Pepi's face remained pressed to the window in silent wonder from the time of rumbling through the Varigotti tunnel until the arrival in Savona, where he looked around quickly at Carlo as if to credit his eyes at the size of the buildings.

"They are even bigger in Genoa," said Carlo, feeling a little silly.

At Albissola Marina fish sandwiches were being sold at the station, and Carlo bought them each one. Pepi munched his happily and almost dropped it in a panic of excitement as the train slid by a scene of pandemonium on the road to Celle Ligure.

"What is it?" He choked and pointed to the waving flags and the sleek, snorting, brightly painted automobiles with their helmeted drivers.

"Only an automobile race."

The cars sped beside the train for a while, gaining speed, amid the cheers and shouts of the passengers, and then disappeared one by one in the distance. Pepi craned his neck to see the last cloud of dust and sighed in ecstasy. Carlo drank some of his wine and hoped there wouldn't be any more excitement.

But this of all days would be the day when there was a festival in Arenzano, with revelers singing and dancing on both sides of the train, and flower-bedecked boats rocking in the tiny Gulf.

"Is it always like this on the train?" asked Pepi breathlessly.

"No," said Carlo. "When we get to Genoa, stay close to me and don't get lost."

"All right," Pepi promised, and he waved at a merry-maker who was swinging a large bell and delighting his companions by sticking out an inordinately red and very large tongue.

"Is that really his tongue?" Pepi wanted to know.

"Of course not," said Carlo. "People don't have tongues like that."

They had passed through Pegli without further event before Pepi spoke again. "You must have been every-where," he said.

"No," said Carlo. "Not quite everywhere."

"Then how do you know there aren't people with tongues like that?"

"I suppose I don't," Carlo admitted. "But you mustn't be rude."

"Is it rude to talk about people's tongues?"

"No. That isn't what I meant."

"Do you like to say some words more than others?" Pepi asked suddenly.

Carlo blinked. "No. I don't think so."

"I do. I like some words. I say them over and over. You say no a lot. Do you like to say no?"

Carlo swallowed and considered several possible an-swers, wondering at the same time how severe he was allowed to be if the occasion demanded.

"No," he said finally.

Pepi looked up at him with a twinkle as though they

had just exchanged a cryptic secret. Carlo frowned back at him sternly, which sent Pepi into a fit of delighted laughter.

Diversion came again with the sprawling, tumbled pile of ancient gray buildings that were Pepi's introduction to Genoa. The teeming, yelling city seemed to unfold with a rising clangor culminating in the roar of the railroad station. Following instructions, Carlo ordered a taxicab, which charged noisily and angrily through hostile crowds that seemed to separate just in time for its passage. Pepi was fascinated by the unending clamor, by the smell of tar and fish and gasoline, and even by the backbreaking cobbled street over which the taxi apparently doubled its careening speed. He stared openmouthed at the forest of ships' spars and listened with delight to the complaining cranes and creaking winches that all but drowned out the shouts of the dock hands. As for the great ship itself, Pepi was unable to utter a syllable while in its vicinity.

They rode a bus back to the station and found they had an hour until traintime.

"What would you like to do?" asked Carlo.

"See everything!" Pepi said eagerly.

Carlo groaned inwardly and took his hand.

Within the hour, through no design except for Pepi's infallible instinct for the streets which would lead to activity, they had seen a dancing bear, which even

Carlo found entertaining, a puppet show at which they both laughed aloud, Carlo startling himself in so doing, a small fire attended in full regalia by the fire department, two minor but ingenious collisions, and a traveling carousel, on which Carlo bought Pepi three rides.

Once on the train and homeward bound, Pepi's head began nodding. "I am sleepy," he announced.

"I shouldn't wonder," said Carlo. "Why don't you go to sleep?"

A few minutes later he realized that Pepi was still struggling to keep his eyes open.

"I thought you were going to sleep."

Pepi yawned. "I'm afraid something will happen and I won't see it."

"Shut your eyes," said Carlo. "If anything happens, I promise to tell you."

Pepi shut his eyes. "Is anything happening?" he asked.

"Not a thing," said Carlo. "Suppose I tell you a story."

Pepi smiled and settled back against the seat. Having promised, Carlo searched his mind for a story.

"There was once a boy in Genoa named Ballila," he began. "He lived there when the Austrians were there, and he didn't like the Austrians any more than anyone else did. . . ."

But Pepi was asleep.

It wasn't this experience in itself that won Carlo to Pepi. He had truthfully enjoyed the day far more than he had expected to, and he had talked more than he ever remembered talking, but it still wasn't the trip that made the difference.

What really counted happened some days later when he met Giorgio in Benozzo's restaurant.

"Pepi had a good time in Genoa," said Giorgio.

"So did I," Carlo replied honestly.

"Of course he made up a lot of things that happened. He is a magnificent liar," Giorgio apologized proudly. "There were dancing bears and a fire and many other things."

"They were all true," said Carlo. A question came to his mind. "What did he enjoy most?"

Giorgio scratched his chin.

"I asked him that, too," he said. "He knew right away. He said, 'Carlo told me a story.'"

Thus it was that Carlo elected himself one of Pepi's fathers.

Regarding all other things, however, he was still considered a notorious skeptic. Whether his dour aspect was the result of inveterate pessimism or whether his pessimism was the result of brooding over his appearance was a topic on which Vittore, at least, liked to hold forth.

"Carlo," Vittore would say, "has convinced himself that he is a man who must have something to worry

68

about. If he has nothing to worry about, this in itself is enough to upset him."

Jacopo was inclined to be more charitable.

"He had an unhappy childhood," he would protest.

"Don't misunderstand me," Vittore would reply. "Carlo may be a cynic, but I shall defend him. I like a man to be what he is completely. And no one can say that Carlo is not a complete cynic."

Vittore being the complete arbiter, Carlo's standing as a cynic was then decided once and for all. His brevity of speech of course lent weight to the theory, and since cynicism is more often than not accepted as bitter truth, he also became somewhat renowned as a realist. In this fashion his reputation came full circle, from that of a man who liked to speak briefly and therefore dealt only in facts to that of a man who dealt only in facts and therefore had need to speak but briefly. No harm came to anyone in the process, and Carlo's stature was, if anything, increased.

"I saw Carlo go past," said Pepi to Giorgio.

"I know. I was talking to him."

"He looked sad."

"Carlo always looks sad."

"But he isn't. Not always. Only this morning he really was."

"What makes you think so?"

Pepi carefully placed the empty raspberry-soda bottle in its receptacle. "Didn't you tell me once he was an orphan?"

Giorgio looked surprised. "Yes. Why?"

"Perhaps that's why he is sad."

Giorgio came around the counter slowly. "Are you sad about . . . being an orphan?"

Pepi's eyes widened. "Me! Of course not. I've got you."

"There is something you want to say," Giorgio accused, trying to sound stern. "What is it?"

"Nothing," said Pepi innocently. He busied himself with the towels.

"Pepi! There are no customers. The towels have already been counted. What do you want to say?"

"Nothing, Giorgio. Really."

"You heard us talking about school? Is that it?"

Pepi thought for a moment. "Did you go to school?" he asked.

"Of course I did. Everybody goes to school."

By now Pepi had succeeded in pushing some of the towels from the counter. He picked them up quickly and began folding them.

"Are you and Maria going to be married?" he asked, folding the topmost towel very deliberately.

Giorgio walked to the front of the veranda and stood

spraddle-legged, his arms folded, looking at the beach. "Why do you ask that?"

There was no answer, and he turned, only to discover Pepi standing beside him, also spraddle-legged, also with his arms folded.

"I don't know," said Pepi, looking at the beach. "I just asked."

"Don't bother your head about things like that," said Giorgio. "Have another raspberry soda."

Chapter five

Vittore

THERE was a single umbrella on the beach. Later in the day there would be hundreds, and the broad, flat slope of sand and gravel between Crena Point and the Cape of Caprazoppa would resemble a crowded bed of giant, varicolored mushrooms, whereas now the impression was more like a flower in the desert.

Pepi pointed to the single umbrella. It was one of Giorgio's, and its stripes were a violent apricot and mauve.

Giorgio nodded. "It's Vittore," he said. "He is being solitary."

This was said entirely without malice. Vittore's periodic solitudes were not at all unusual, and no one would be so disloyal as to suggest that they were also frequently conspicuous. A stranger once hinted that Vittore's methods of seeking privacy were a bit dramatic, if not ostentatious. He was met immediately with spirited arguments to the contrary.

"An ordinary man," proclaimed Benozzo, with his mustache at a lofty angle, "uses no imagination when he wants to be alone. He locks himself in a room or creeps off into the hills. There is nothing so furtive about Vittore. When he isolates himself he does it with boldness!"

"There is a difference," Carlo said briefly, "between ostentation and simple emphasis."

"Exactly!" said Giorgio. "Vittore is a man of endless talents. Is it so strange that he has a talent for *looking* alone as well as *being* alone?"

Even Jacopo had an opinion. "Vittore is generous with his solitude," he reasoned. "He shares it with us."

And nothing more needed to be said on the subject.

The temper of an antagonist usually determined Vittore's mood; he matched stubbornness with sternness, wit with whimsy, wile with guile. Thus it was that he contemplated the submissive sea lapping near his feet with warm benignity. In this aspect he was a smallish, square man sitting on a folding chair, undistinguished except for the fact that he wore a coat. In actual appearance you might even say that he was far less likely to attract attention than Giorgio, who was handsomer, Jacopo, who was rounder and smaller, Benozzo, who was more massive, or Carlo, who was thinner.

If you met him a second or third time, however, you would correct yourself in surprise and wonder how it was possible to make such a mistake. For Vittore sitting quietly under an umbrella communing with the sea was one thing and Vittore at any other time was quite another. If you saw him championing a point of logic, for example, you would swear he was a heavy man. And if you observed him in a really heated argument, you would note with amazement that he was surely the tallest person in the room, with blazing eyes and an astonishingly long forefinger. On his bicycle he was a figure of punishing wrath, pedaling relentlessly in wide arcs, oblivious of the cowardly vehicles that wavered or toppled out of his way. Then again, on a fast day, no one in Father Luigi's flock would look more pinched and self-denying, even emaciated.

In all manifestations, though, he wore his coat. It was his emblem, his insigne of authority. Even in his own tiny garden on the hottest day of the year his only concession to the heat would be to loosen his black string tie and unfasten the top button of his shirt.

It would be too easy to dispose of Vittore by saying he was a philosopher. He was, by his own indirect admission, also a theologian, a musician and gourmet. He could answer any question on navigation, meteorology or donkeys. He had been known to identify a bird which to no one else was more than a speck in the sky, and if challenged he could quote the bird's Latin name to prove it. He was an expert on politics, sea shells and chess. He discussed the iron mine with the air of a former mineralogist, the foundry as a former engineer, the new post office as a former architect. Carlo, a cynic even in admiration, declared that he discussed women with the assurance of a former woman.

Vittore was not a native of Finale Ligure. He had arrived one day, many years past, with a valise full of books in his bicycle basket and a government pension from an obscure source. He was vague about himself but startlingly precise on almost any other subject. Benozzo, being of an orderly turn of mind, once made a calculation based on Vittore's admitted or implied careers.

"The way I figure it, he'd be two hundred and sixteen years old," he told Giorgio.

And yet it was Benozzo who became Vittore's first stanch friend in Finale Ligure.

It was because of the affair of the coffin stones.

There were several hundred of them, and they had no connection with coffins or even cemeteries. They were simply large stone blocks left over because of some miscalculation in the plans for the new post office. For three or four weeks they lay in a disordered pile and were quickly nicknamed coffin stones by the children because of the uneven oblong shape, being slightly wider at one end than at the other.

Benozzo eyed them hungrily for a while and estimated that with just about twelve of them he could realize a long-felt dream. Six of the heavy stones piled neatly at either end of his restaurant front would separate the sidewalk portion of his property from the basketmaker's display on one side (there were always innuendos about wine stains from careless diners) and the cobbler shop on the other. He would have, in effect, a walled terrazza. Maybe even a potted plant on the top of each wall. . . .

He went to Signor Ghigliamo, the mayor.

"What is going to be done with the stones by the post office?" he asked tentatively.

"You're the fifth one to make a complaint about them!" Signor Ghigliamo groaned, chewing unhappily on a pencil. "I know . . . I know! They're unsightly and they ruin the appearance of the new post office! I wish somebody would tell *me* what to do with them!"

"I can take a few of them off your hands," Benozzo suggested hopefully.

"No, no, it's impossible."

"Why?" Benozzo wondered.

"I'd be glad to help you if I could," said the mayor. "But God knows, it's enough of a tangle already! The stones were bought—out of our quarries, of course—by the American government as a gift. Now our government owns them for a post office."

"But the post office is already built!"

"*I* know that and *you* know it but . . . the plans . . ." He discarded his chewed pencil and made a halfhearted move toward the sea of papers on his desk. "Anyway, there are plans. Specifications—very official. And according to them there are no stones left over!"

"But there are! I saw them."

The mayor selected a fresh pencil and bit it as if it were a breadstick.

"Benozzo," he said sadly, "in public life one cannot see what one looks at but only what is official!"

"There were trucks going away all the time," Benozzo pointed out.

"Yes, carrying parts of the old post office. They were asked to take the . . . ah . . . coffin stones, and the drivers —quite properly—refused. There was no removal order."

"The Americans——" began Benozzo, who was beginning to forget his own project in concern for the mayor's quandary.

"No good!" Signor Ghigliamo shook his head dolefully. "The stones were given as a free gift, and the

77

American authorities—again properly—do not wish to make a bad appearance by taking back part of their gift."

Benozzo's mustache went to work. After a moment he leaned conspiratorially over the mayor's desk.

"If some night . . . after it became quite dark . . ."

He paused meaningfully.

"Please, Benozzo!" The mayor placed a hand quickly over his heart. "You truly alarm me! No . . . no, it is out of the question! I cannot permit the stones to be moved from the post-office premises except by processes both legal and ethical!"

"But you just said there are no such processes!"

"Precisely," said the mayor, spitting out pieces of pencil. "No, no cigar, thank you. I have given up smoking. It makes me nervous."

Later in his restaurant Benozzo recounted this interview to Jacopo and Giorgio. Three men were playing cards garrulously at a corner table, and one guest sat with his back to the counter, drinking coffee.

When Benozzo had finished, the coffee drinker stood up slowly and walked toward Benozzo. It was Vittore.

"Pardon me," he said. "These stones you speak of. How much do they weigh?"

Benozzo looked at Giorgio and Jacopo. "About seven chilos," he said finally.

"And how many would you like to have?"

"I might as well want all of them," Benozzo mourned, "instead of only twelve. Excuse me, however, your back was turned. Maybe you didn't understand the impossibility——"

"It is a matter," Vittore said calmly, "requiring a certain amount of ingenuity. May I offer my services?"

Benozzo again consulted Giorgio and Jacopo. Giorgio shrugged. Jacopo quivered excitedly.

"I shall need," said Vittore, anticipating Benozzo's nod, "a large piece of heavy paper. Also a small amount of money."

"Camouflage!" exclaimed Giorgio.

"Bribery . . . ?" said Jacopo dubiously.

Vittore held up a restraining hand.

"Neither camouflage nor bribery," he said. "Merely removal by due legal process. Removal by the very authorities who are undoubtedly most concerned. I have had some small experience," he added modestly, "with literal application of the law."

"This is not exactly an affair of the law," Benozzo began.

"So much the better." Vittore nodded.

There was a pause.

"I have a small amount of money," said Giorgio.

"And I will find a large piece of heavy paper," said Benozzo.

Thirty minutes later, having left Tonio in charge of

the restaurant, the four men arrived at the post office. Vittore stood critically beside the pile of coffin stones.

"This one," he said finally.

Giorgio, following instructions willingly but with silent doubt, wrapped the heavy stone in the paper.

"A piece of cord," said Vittore.

Jacopo sought among the inevitable bystanders who had gathered and returned with a suitable length of twine, which Giorgio tied around the paper.

Vittore inspected the work and nodded approvingly. "Now bring the stone and follow me," he instructed.

As the bystanders watched and speculated Vittore led the way into the post office.

"Here," he said, and Giorgio placed the package in front of the caged window.

"Contents?" asked the attendant, yawning.

"Building materials," Vittore replied, scribbling Benozzo's address on the paper.

The attendant yawned again, opened his grilled window and pulled the package through.

"Heavy," he grunted complainingly as he struggled with the scales. "Two hundred lire."

Giorgio counted out the money, and the four men turned away solemnly.

"Now what?" asked Benozzo.

"We shall need another piece of paper and two hundred lire," said Vittore as they walked down the steps.

It was while the fifth stone was being mailed that the post-office attendant became wary.

"How long is this going on?" he wanted to know.

Giorgio dug into his pocket ruefully. He had five hundred-lire notes. "Not very long," he said.

The attendant slammed the window. "Wait a minute," he said, disappearing.

"There is . . . no one watching my cabanas," Giorgio remembered aloud.

"There are deliveries of cheese to be made," said Jacopo uncomfortably.

"Tonio is sure to break half the glasses in the restaurant," said Benozzo, looking nervously at the closed window. "It would be better if I went back."

Vittore alone was unperturbed. He straightened his black string tie carefully and smoothed his coat front.

"I'll come with you," he said. "I think I would like some more coffee."

The mayor's neck was very red as he paced up and down Benozzo's restaurant. His tone was half angry, half reproachful.

"If only you had consulted me first," he was saying, "I would have explained to you that it was impossible!"

"Excuse me," Vittore interposed mildly. "But the authorities——"

"I am the authorities!" said the mayor unhappily.

"And I am placed in a very embarrassing predicament."

Vittore clucked sympathetically. "It may be possible for me to help," he offered.

There was no confidence in Signor Ghigliamo's somewhat baleful eye.

"I was about to remark," Vittore went on, "that the authorities—including mayors—are in the habit of relying on precedents in such cases."

"Well?" There was a note of suspicious challenge.

"The precedent in the case has been established. The packages were accepted for mailing."

The mayor seemed on the point of exploding.

"Eugh," he said. "Mmmff!"

Benozzo polished his counter unnecessarily and watched Vittore.

The mayor searched his pockets in vain for a pencil. "The stones were not to be removed from the premises," he said painfully.

"They were not removed from the premises by us," Vittore pointed out with perfect logic. "If the postal authorities see fit to remove them as pieces of mail, that is their responsibility. In fact, it is now their duty."

"Most unfortunately true," the mayor agreed, searching through his pockets a second time. "Do you," he asked desperately, "have a pencil?"

Benozzo handed him one, and he thrust it between his teeth gratefully.

"You *wanted* the stones removed," Benozzo reminded. "Our action was really in the nature of a service to the community."

"And," added Vittore comfortably, "eventually to the people all over Italy who can find a use for stones of such proportions."

"All over Italy!" The mayor choked as the pencil broke in two. "My . . . my dear friend, I appeal to you. The talk . . . the—" he shivered slightly—"laughter!"

Vittore placed the ends of his fingers together and thought.

Suddenly he seemed inspired. "But if the act were an official one," he suggested.

The mayor straightened in his chair. "Official?"

"Let us consider the facts," said Vittore. "First, removing the stones was an impossibility. Second, there was an ingenious solution. Third, this solution was invented and executed by—" he bowed—"the resourceful mayor of Finale Ligure."

The mayor looked from Vittore to Benozzo.

"Official," he repeated. "The . . . the postage . . ."

"Two hundred lire for each stone," said Vittore idly.

Signor Ghigliamo trembled. "There are . . . hundreds of them," he said. "The town can never stand the expense."

Vittore looked concerned.

"What a shame!" he said. "Stories like this unfortunately get around very quickly. People will wonder why the town doesn't seize on this chance to remove an obstacle to civic beauty."

The mayor groaned. "If only I had overlooked the legalities in the first place!" he grieved. "A truck at night, an abandoned quarry up in the hills . . . but of course it was unthinkable."

Vittore eyed him sympathetically and said nothing.

Signor Ghigliamo rose unsteadily to his feet.

"However," he said, "it is ungrateful of me not to thank you for your interest. You will excuse me? There are . . . certain things to be done."

The night following this colloquy was the one during which residents in the neighborhood of the new post office complained of a good deal of unnecessary noise—a truck motor, the thuds and scrapes of heavy objects, the grunts of men carrying burdens. An anonymous observer who peeked through the blinds thought (though he admitted he must be mistaken) that the driver of the truck bore a remarkable resemblance to Mayor Ghigliamo.

There were two interesting side effects of the episode. One was that, by a most peculiar chance, seven coffin-shaped stones (for the coffin stones were never seen again after that night) apparently slipped off the truck when it was making the difficult turn on the Piazza XXV Aprile directly in front of Benozzo's restaurant. The other was that Vittore and Benozzo became inseparable friends.

It followed then that Giorgio and Jacopo, too, fell into the habit of consulting Vittore regarding any decision of moment. Carlo alone was inclined to be skeptical until the day Vittore showed him how to save fourteen steps while carrying luggage from the sidewalk to the Hotel elevator.

It was also natural that Vittore was among the first to be informed of Pepi's advent on the hillside. They were friends from the start, serving each other in many secret ways. Pepi, for instance, could sense when Vittore's meditation periods were about to end and somehow be on hand to fold the gaudy umbrella and carry the small chair back to the cabana. Vittore's reciprocations were more subtle.

On last St. John's Day, for example. With the inevitable eagerness of a small boy to join in the older boys' games, Pepi had breathlessly explored every nook and corner of Finale Ligure for scraps of wood to add to the giant bonfire. Daily the pyramid of broken furniture, crates, discarded baskets, even, regrettably, some stolen lumber grew to impressive proportions on the bank of the Sciusa where the dry river bed crossed the beach, every piece discovered with victorious shouts in an alley or doorway just seconds before Pepi's shorter legs brought him on the scene.

It became almost an obsession with him. To discover

one scrap of wood that he himself might fling on the mighty pyre, to chance on a single barrel stave in a forgotten cranny that had been overlooked by the older boys. But it was not to be. St. John's Day arrived, and Pepi's face seemed as long as his legs were short. To add to his disappointment, with only precious hours remaining before the great blaze would be set off, Vittore sent word that he had chosen to walk home and would like to have Pepi deliver his bicycle.

The bicycle was too big for Pepi, and it meant pushing it ignominiously through streets where bands of shouting boys still pounced on loosened tailboards, drooping blinds (which they reasoned would soon fall off of their own accord) and a box of chewed pencil stubs placed invitingly on the doorstep of the Casa Municipale. Benozzo's neighbor, the basketmaker, had wisely withdrawn his display for several days past.

Vittore had settled down in a small, flat-topped house in the old section of Varigotti. The house formerly had been the gardener's quarters in a handsome villa. On ordinary occasions Pepi liked nothing better than to trudge through the overgrown garden where invisible dragons must surely lurk, skirt with a shiver of delicious terror the forbidding round tower in the corner of the wall and visit the tiny house itself, where there were always sweets hidden in the least likely places.

Today, however, it was different. The garden held no

charmed mysteries, and he walked straight past the tower without noticing it. St. John's Day came only once a year, and the prospect of merely *seeing* the bonfire was a poor substitute for the thrill of watching the flames engulf a box or a board or a stick of his very own.

There was still a little time, although his hopes had almost vanished. He propped the bicycle beside the green door and wondered how he could apologize for not coming in to search for sweets. And then, as Vittore opened the door, his heart skipped a beat. For Vittore held in his hand a superbly demolished chair!

"I was about to throw it out," explained Vittore. "Perhaps you wouldn't mind taking care of it for me."

Pepi nodded, his eyes shining, and took the chair eagerly in both his arms. It was far clumsier than a bicycle, and threatened to fall apart at every other step, and yet the long trip back to the bank of the Sciusa was a flight of joy. That the same chair had been undamaged the day before and now appeared to have been loosened piece by piece and stamped on in the bargain was to him nothing more than an appropriate miracle, and he could certainly be excused for failing to notice that Vittore was slightly lame when he opened the door.

The St. John's Day fires were superlative that year, and everyone agreed that the blaze on the Sciusa bank was the grandest of them all. There was one particularly brilliant cascade of flames which drew cries of admiration from the spectators and which Pepi never doubted was caused by the noble disintegration of the chair he had placed there with his own hands.

Giorgio felt it was his duty at bedtime that night to ask Pepi what he had learned in church and during the day about St. John. He was dismayed by the answer.

"St. John was a very great saint," murmured Pepi drowsily. "He always wore a coat."

Chapter six

Maria

THIS time it was Giorgio instead of Pepi who came to lower the umbrella and carry Vittore's chair back to the cabana.

"Good morning," Giorgio said tentatively.

Vittore looked up. "There is something on your mind," he said.

Giorgio admitted that there was.

"When there is something on my mind," Vittore said, "I concentrate on the opposite and think backward until I encounter the solution."

"I can't think backward," said Giorgio.

"It requires a certain degree of skill," Vittore admitted. "Is it a complex problem or a simple one?"

"I think it is a complex one."

"Then we shall look on the simple side of it. If it were a simple one, we should have to consider the complex side, which is a longer process."

Giorgio dropped on the sand and traced a figure eight slowly with his finger.

"I don't understand that," he said uneasily. He supposed that people of Vittore's intellect had to talk in riddles the way athletes had to exercise, but he wished it made him feel less like a guilty schoolboy who had failed to prepare his lesson.

"Never mind," said Vittore kindly. "What is the problem?"

"They think Pepi should be adopted."

"They?"

"Benozzo. Jacopo. Carlo, I think."

Vittore looked at him and waited. Then he said, "Is there someone else who thinks so?"

"Someone else?" Giorgio's eyebrows went up questioningly.

"So far you have brought me no news. Benozzo, Jacopo, Carlo—you, too—we all agreed Pepi should be adopted."

Giorgio opened his mouth.

"We agreed," Vittore went on, "that a small boy should have a mother."

"Even Father Luigi thinks so."

There was a long pause. Early bathers were beginning

90

to drift out on the beach. Giorgio glanced automatically toward the veranda where Pepi was dispensing bathhouse keys with brisk assurance. He drew a circle in the sand around the figure eight.

"Why don't you ask Maria?" said Vittore finally.

"Maria?" Giorgio's startled tone implied that undoubtedly there *was* such a person as Maria but that her connection with the topic was remote if not nonexistent.

"Why don't you ask her?" Vittore repeated.

Giorgio sighed. There was no use trying to deceive a man who looked straight down through the top of your head into your very thoughts. "Benozzo says a woman would not like to be the mother of a six-year-old boy on her wedding day."

"A woman," said Vittore, getting up and bending his head so as to avoid striking the rim of the umbrella, "becomes the mother of a full-grown man on her wedding day. It is a knowledge shared by all women, whereas being a *wife* is a private adventure. That is why there is a bond among mothers but none among wives."

Giorgio was puzzled. "Then what will Maria say?"

"She will say one thing with her lips, another with her eyes and still another with her heart. And, Giorgio . . ."

"Yes?"

"This is the secret of knowing a woman. All three will be the truth."

Vittore smiled and walked off toward the cabana as

Giorgio struggled to his feet, his forehead like corduroy.

"Riddles!" he said under his breath to the umbrella and furled it in two angry motions as if it had attempted to argue.

Benozzo had once said that the whole of Finale Ligure was one huge thermometer. If one measured from the beach back to the hills, the heat of the day could be judged by where signs of life stopped. On a hot day the workers on the hillside would slow to a mere hint of movement, cyclists and pedestrians on the street would seek the shady side of buildings and one fugitive after another, unfastening his clinging shirt as he went, would drift to the transplanted town of umbrellas and vagrant breezes by the ocean.

Today whatever life existed in the high, shelflike olive and poplar groves had melted into the shadows of trees; donkeys stood stock-still, as though carved out of the mountain; in the town proper, green shutters creaked shut, canvas store fronts hung motionless and the only sound was the fitful groan of ceiling fans within. Even the palmettos along the elegant Via Aurelia drooped in sad reproach. Not a person in motion could be seen except on the beach.

"Even to think," Benozzo would have said, "is a mistake on such a day. One's thoughts will be scorched."

Giorgio, however, was a man of conventional pattern. Having started the day by thinking, he found it impossible to turn off his brain, even though the heat seemed to burn right into his reflections. Customers, cash register, ice chest of soft drinks and grappa—these were matters he could handle automatically, even as Pepi automatically counted umbrellas and retrieved empty bottles. But his thoughts—they defied the sun, arithmetic and professional demeanor. They rolled and crashed and collided in his head. They were formless and turbulent—of Pepi, schoolbooks, Vittore, Americans, Maria. . . .

Maria! He was suddenly overcome by a new realization. Until this day he had never considered himself in love, and yet here he was mooning over everything in terms of a girl's opinion. Was this the way it happened? Did you go along for months and years making perfectly sensible decisions and then abruptly become incapable of a coherent thought? Did you depend on your strong back in the iron mines and your good business head in the cabanas and in a single day discredit both?

And if he was in love with Maria, which now seemed as obvious as it was unexpected, which Maria was he in love with? The Maria whose anger broke like a summer storm over a small injustice? The Maria who would dance with you on a Friday night as if you were the only person in the world and go sailing with someone else Saturday morning as if you didn't exist? The roguish one who looked at you with merry, unfathomable eyes and told you you were too serious when you wanted to talk, too frivolous when you tried to kiss her? The grave beauty who listened to every word of the Mass with her gloved hands folded in her lap? Or the barefoot tomboy who flew through her father's olive grove with skirt tucked above her knees?

Were these the attributes of a mother? He remembered Pepi's first encounter with Maria a year ago, when she curiously peeped in at the cabana veranda.

"Where is Giorgio?" she asked.

"Out there," Pepi said without hesitation, pointing to a lateen-rigged sailboat becalmed offshore. "The pirates caught him."

"That's too bad," she replied solemnly. "I expect they'll eat him alive."

Giorgio stood up, flushed, behind the counter where he had been searching for a lost key.

"Is that any way to talk to a small boy?" he demanded.

She tossed her black head. "*Somebody* is going to be eaten alive," she retorted. "Somebody who promised to take a girl to the cinema last night and never came."

"Jacopo gave Pepi a goat," he explained. "I was building a pen for him. We'll go to the cinema tonight."

"Tonight," she said loftily, "you may go to the cinema with the goat!" And she stalked off with a switch of her red skirt.

"Besides," she called back from the street, "someone else took me."

Of course her anger hadn't lasted. It never seemed to. But he did know that there was always "someone else." Even today, long after Pepi and Maria had become first cautious friends and later giggling conspirators, he had a disquieting knowledge that there were a dozen young men whose thoughts of Maria were uncomplicated with little boys.

For that matter, what right did he have to think that she would marry him with or without Pepi? Why Giorgio the slow-witted who could not understand logic or philosophy? Why Giorgio the tongue-tied who managed to think of things to say for every other occasion and went dumb the moment he arrived at Maria's door? Why Giorgio the idiot who built goat pens when the most beautiful girl in Finale Ligure waited for him? Why Giorgio at all? he asked himself fiercely.

What girl in her right mind would choose a blockhead who spent the summer in the broiling sun and the winter in a hole in the ground! And dreaming at both, he added, feeling less of a man by the minute. Dreaming now when he should be checking the bathhouses to make sure their users had remembered to lock them. Dreaming last February in the mine, or he wouldn't have been caught by that premature blast.

All those hours of digging through the night for stupid, napping Giorgio, who was perfectly safe and comfortable every minute and feeling nothing but ashamed for the trouble he was causing. He remembered the relieved shouts of the diggers when he climbed sheepishly through the hole. And he remembered Pepi's tear-stained face and glad cry and the owlish faces of what seemed like hundreds of people peering grayly through the fire-lit early dawn. All his friends, almost everyone he knew—except Maria Bonelli.

He saw her that night, and they joked about the expense he had caused by getting trapped and about how the ore would have been dented if it had struck his head. And it wasn't until three days later that he learned from Father Luigi where she had been, kneeling throughout the night at the feet of the Virgin's statue in the unheated church, protected only by her mother's large shawl over her head. All right, he told himself, but she is a warm-hearted, virtuous girl. She would have done the same for any friend.

At any rate, neither he nor Maria ever seemed to talk of these things. Or of Pepi. He had started to speak during the last Carnevale when they were teaching Pepi the children's games. It was Maria, her eyes dancing, who blindfolded Pepi, put the stick in his hand and held the other children back as she guided him, slashing wildly, to the swinging earthen pot with its treasure of nuts and sweets. And then when the pot broke with a glorious crunch, and the sweets tumbled all over the floor of the Bonellis' tasseled parlor, she was romping and laughing like one of the children, fighting for a share of the spoils.

"It's like having a baby brother," she told Giorgio, sweeping her hair breathlessly out of her eyes and offering him a mashed nougat. And somehow, whatever Giorgio was going to say seemed ill-timed.

But Vittore and Benozzo were right. Now was the time to stop thinking and . . . act? Well, no, but talk, at least. So he started formulating a speech.

At first, the direct appeal.

"Maria," he would say, "some American friends of Jacopo's are coming next Tuesday, and . . ."

No, that was wrong. They were not truthfully friends of Jacopo's. And next Tuesday was five days off. At lunch, munching farinata with Pepi on the cabana steps, he decided that it would be much wiser to put off a discussion with Maria for another day or two.

In the afternoon, directing some English people to the Hotel where they could rent a boat, he wrinkled his forehead over another approach.

"Maria, Pepi is very fond of you. . . ."

But was that the truth? Did he *know* what Pepi thought of Maria? It was one thing to be a friendly playmate to a girl who thought of you as a little brother and quite a different thing to imagine her scrubbing your face and making you do your lessons and scolding you when you tracked in dirt and goat hairs. Quite a different thing to imagine her married to your . . . to your what?

"I'm not even his father!" he exclaimed aloud.

"Pardon?" said one of the English people.

He felt the back of his neck getting red under the tan.

"I'm sorry," he said in English. "I was thinking of my little boy."

There was a glance exchanged which said as plainly in English as in Italian, "You never know about these southern people!"

By the end of the day he had thought of an entirely new beginning.

"Maria, it is time for Pepi to have a mother. . . ."

It wasn't a very romantic way to ask for a girl's hand, but Maria was a levelheaded person—except when she was angry—and there was certainly nothing to make her angry in such a simple statement.

He furled the last umbrella and gave Pepi a five-hundred-lire note for the early picture at the cinema.

"Benozzo will give you something to eat," he said.

"Aren't you going to eat?"

"Perhaps later."

"With Maria?" Giorgio wasn't sure whether the tone was suspicious or merely curious.

"Never mind. Hurry or you'll be late. It's an American picture—about cowboys."

"May I come with you instead?"

"No! I have important business."

Pepi fingered the five-hundred-lire note.

"If I can get in through the side door may I keep the money?"

Giorgio was shocked. "Of course not! You're to go in the front door and buy a ticket, or I'll see that you're tan in the one place you're not! Now run."

"Bang! Bang!" said Pepi, scurrying off toward Benozzo's.

It was still light. Giorgio walked slowly toward the Piazza XXV Aprile, where a band in fine yellow uniforms was tuning up for a concert. He bought a bunch of flowers, laughed with the other spectators as one of the musicians tried to chase a dog away with his trombone, started across the Square toward the street leading steeply upward to the Bonellis' house, and five minutes later dropped the flowers in a wire trash basket on the street, turned abruptly and walked in the opposite direction.

Since the hillside path to his own small house lay westward, he found himself crossing the Square again, with the concert in full voice. Dusk was falling now, and a light breeze caressed the trees on the avenue. Shutters that had been clamped tight during the day were beginning to pop outward, as if pried open by the brassy blasts of the band.

The music was comforting. Its raucous clamor made it

impossible to think. He leaned against a corner of the Spanish Arch and let the blaring of the trumpets fill his head. Somewhere in Benozzo's restaurant across the Square Pepi was gorging on spaghetti. Somewhere on the darkening hillside Maria was sitting at a window listening to the music or sewing on her youngest sister's confirmation dress or talking her father out of discharging a lazy Piedmontese donkey driver who was bewitching the olives.

His imaginary picture of Maria at home was so convincing that when she walked up to him he started.

"Maria!" he said guiltily.

She smiled, and almost as if the music had been scored for her arrival the trumpets stopped and the woodwinds began a muted, low-register passage. Her black hair shone softly in the light of the street lamp as she nodded.

"I was sure you'd forget to be here," she said. "You're always forgetting things lately."

Forgot! Again! He looked so chagrined that she quickly took his hand.

"All right, you needn't look so offended. I was only teasing!" Then, seeing the telltale furrows in his forehead, she leaned toward him anxiously. "Giorgio, you're worried about something!"

"Me?" he said in a tone of surprise.

But she wasn't satisfied. "Come, tell me about it."

She took his arm and led him across the drowsing avenue away from the band, which instantly tried to overtake them with a surge of deafening volume.

"We can't talk here!" he shouted.

"We'll go down on the beach," she said, steering him expertly by the elbow.

Giorgio the woodenhead, he thought as he fell awkwardly into step with her. Forgetting a promise to meet Maria at the concert. Throwing away a thousand lire's worth of flowers. Letting everyone, including Maria, decide when he must talk to her. They walked down the stone steps and out onto the sand where the ocean saluted the pale twilight with a sibilant whisper.

They stopped only when they reached the water's edge. The quiet sea was faintly luminous, the town behind them a gem-crusted necklace, and there was the never-ending miracle that the mountains seemed to follow them instead of receding and to swell visibly higher into the fast-darkening sky. Giorgio felt slightly giddy—whether from the night, the light pressure of Maria's hand on his arm or the subtle aura of her perfume he wasn't sure.

He glanced at her almost shyly, then turned quickly away. Although Maria's face was only a soft blur in the darkness, he felt that his own look of hopeless confusion must be as clear as an electric sign.

"What is it, caro?" she asked quietly. "You are so serious, so sober tonight."

"I . . . was thinking of Pepi," he said clumsily and immediately swore at himself as her hand dropped from his arm. "I mean of Pepi and you," he added honestly.

"Which of us has been naughty?" she asked in a voice that might be teasing—or gently sarcastic.

"Neither of you, of course!" he said uncomfortably. "That is . . . well, Pepi isn't *always* good."

She waited in silence. Somewhere on the beach a pair of lovers laughed. The throb of a passing motor blended with the band music, and far in the distance a train whistle bleated sadly.

"If he were," Giorgio went on, trying not to stumble over his words, "perhaps one of the American families might have adopted him."

She still didn't reply.

"I guess nobody wants him," he said, staring hard at the ocean. It seemed as if his breathing must surely be louder than the band. "Of course it may be different with Jacopo's friends."

He could feel her turn toward him. "Jacopo's friends?"

"More Americans. They are coming Tuesday." He drew a deep breath. "Father Luigi thinks Pepi should have a mother. Vittore thinks so too."

But she was silent again.

"Benozzo says that Pepi could learn a trade in an orphanage."

Maria sighed. "And what do you say?" she asked finally.

"Me?"

"Yes. What does Giorgio say?"

He looked at his feet, shapeless shadows on the sand.

"I don't want Pepi to go to an orphanage. But it isn't for me to say."

"*What* isn't for you to say?"

"Why, whether Pepi should go to an orphanage or be adopted by Jacopo's Americans or . . . or something else."

"Something else, Giorgio?"

"That is . . . if there *were* something else," he suggested hopefully. "If one of us were to marry . . . I mean, Vittore or Carlo or . . . or maybe me."

"*Is* Vittore going to marry?" she asked, and he recognized an edge on her voice that indicated trouble. "Or Carlo? Or . . . maybe you?"

"I wouldn't marry anyone but . . . you," he said lamely, and then realized to his amazement that the crucial words were out. "I mean—naturally it's up to you!"

"Is it?" she flared. "Are you sure it isn't up to Vittore or Carlo or Benozzo or Giuseppe the peachgrower or Toto the cinema star or——"

103

"Maria . . . Maria, please," he begged. "I'm only asking you to . . . to marry me! You don't have to tell me tonight. Perhaps . . . tomorrow."

She started walking away. "I shall be busy tomorrow."

Giorgio nearly stumbled in his haste to catch up with her. "Then the next day."

"The next day I shall be even busier!"

"But . . . Maria. Listen to me. I know I didn't say it very well, but . . . ."

She stopped abruptly and whirled to face him, her hands on her hips and her feet wide apart in the sand.

"When did you say the Americans are coming?"

"On Tuesday."

"Then I'll answer you on Wednesday."

Suddenly the band seemed shrill and discordant, until Giorgio realized it was a crashing in his own ears. The mountains seemed to slip away, the beach became unsteady.

"Does that mean . . . if things are different on Wednesday?"

"It means, Giorgio Cappelletti," she said fiercely, "that when I am married—*if* I marry—it will be to a man and not to a . . . a committee! And it also means that the man will not be one who is so afraid of hurting one person that he hurts another even more! And it means most

104

of all that I shall certainly not marry a man who asks me to make his decisions for him!"

And suddenly she was gone, leaving only a lingering fragrance and the ring of her words.

Giorgio stood frozen for a moment, then turned and walked slowly, blindly back toward the water. The worst of his fears had become reality. It was plain that he must decide between Maria and Pepi. Or *was* it plain? Was anything plain when a woman said it? Was anything plain in all the world except that Giorgio had the tongue of a donkey and the brain of a goat!

The band had stopped playing briefly, and from the open door of the cinema he heard the familiar thunder of racing hoofs and the racketing of guns. The shouts of the audience were, as usual, irrelevant to the drama— except for one unmistakable voice, piping a continuous and approving "Bang, bang, bang!"

Chapter seven

The Americans

To all appearances, Tuesday was a day like any other, a blue-and-gold day in a seemingly endless succession of blue-and-gold days. Two bougainvillea buds opened on the rooftop terrazza of Signor Veneto, the architect. Father Luigi officiated at two weddings, one funeral and a soccer game. Fortunato's horse, after eleven years of letting passers-by pluck carobs and feed them to him, discovered for the first time that he could nibble them off the trees himself.

Emilio, whose job was to tend the drying racks in the pasta factory, sang an aria from *The Barber of Seville* with such volume and gusto that a passing policeman stuck his head in to make sure no one had got hurt by falling into the machinery. A bright-red bus bound for a flower festival in Imperia collided with a bright-red bus bound for a boat race in Savona with the result that the passengers, who left their respective vehicles instantly on being told to remain seated, became somewhat mixed up when they re-embarked and in half a dozen cases attended the wrong event.

Giusti Bergamo, who operated an automobile service station and for whom no day was complete without at least one gambling venture, challenged a French tourist on the relative merits of a Peugeot and a Fiat. They repaired to Benozzo's restaurant to settle the issue over a bottle of grappa. An hour later Giusti graciously conceded and permitted the Frenchman, as winner, to pay for the grappa.

These were normal events, a part of the daily rhythm. But there were others, subtle deviations from routine, that betrayed the special significance of the day for Benozzo, who spent an unusual amount of time at the front of his restaurant, puffing thoughtful clouds of cigar smoke and staring speculatively at passing cars, particularly American ones. For Jacopo, whose sisters ran him out of the cheese factory after breakfast in the fear that his state of excitement would be harmful to the ricotta. For Giorgio, who undertook with seeming absent-mindedness all the early-morning tasks that would ordinarily be Pepi's and performed them with desperate slowness, as if he could thus retard the passing of time.

And for Carlo, whose actions were the most amazing of all. In the exercise of his special talent, economy of effort, he ordinarily resisted a summons to carry luggage until repeated cries assured him that his ears had not deceived him and that no one else was available. On this day, however, Signor Resta, the manager of the Hotel, having opened his mouth to bellow for a porter, left it open in pure astonishment, for the mere sound of a stopping automobile brought Carlo loping aggressively to the door.

This happened several times during the morning, to Signor Resta's increasing alarm. Carlo's performance for every arriving party consisted of an appraising stare, a shrug and an immediate retreat to the sanctuary of the elevator, where he waited for the customary series of summonses.

Since most of the visitors stopped only for breakfast, to ask directions or to cash a travel check, his activities produced little more than a mental collection of turisti, whom from long experience he was able to classify quickly.

The chattering French family, who would return to France with everything imaginable—menus, ash trays, candle stubs, sea shells and empty wine bottles. The stoical Swiss family, who brought everything imaginable with them—soap, cheese, buttons, small stove and earthenware pan, pills to combat the effects of non-Swiss water, food and wine. The Englishman whose sole largess would be Players cigarettes. The American bridegroom who tipped too lavishly, and his bride who noted the fact with timid resolve to bring about later reforms. The other American couple whose expressions of beady disdain suggested that they should have had breakfast in Alassio, where she wanted to, or in Imperia, where he wanted to, whereas here they were in Finale Whatever-It-Is, a social breach that could never be properly explained back home.

After several of Carlo's silent visitations at the door, the manager finally interposed himself.

"There are," he said, "elections about almost everything in Italy these days."

Disagreement being pointless and agreement being superfluous, Carlo was respectfully silent.

"It could be possible," continued Signor Resta, "that you are conducting a private election of a patron worthy to have his bag carried or his automobile door opened. I only mention it because if you are expecting Saint Peter, he is much more likely to stop at the Basilica than here."

But Carlo was no longer listening. Over Signor Resta's shoulder he had caught sight of a fat, open American car nosing its way cautiously to the curb. In it were a pleasant-looking man and woman who nodded to each other as they read the Hotel sign. He walked down the steps and opened the automobile door.

"Sometimes," said Signor Resta to himself, "these little talks are very fruitful."

The American woman smiled at Carlo, and her husband handed him the key to the luggage compartment.

"Do you speak English?" he asked, in English.

Signor Resta bounded down the steps and waved Carlo aside. "Of excellence, Commendatore!" He beamed.

"Ah, good. We have a room here, I believe. The name is Clune."

Carlo judged the man to be about thirty-two, the woman a little younger. He approved the automobile, the matched suitcases and the generous width of the back seat, large enough for Pepi to stretch out full length in the event of any late driving.

By the time he reached the lobby with two of the suitcases, Signor Resta was demonstrating his entire English vocabulary. The last American to stay at the Hotel having been a boxer, the conversation was richly colored with references to uppercuts, palookas and split decisions. The American Commendatore was learning that the Hotel restaurant would serve luncheon at the bell of eleven-thirty and that to see Finale Ligure one needed a guide who was on the ropes.

"A small boy," Carlo suggested quickly, in English.

Signor Clune turned to him.

"Thanks," he said, "but we have a friend here. That is,

110

a friend of a friend. We're going to try to find him after we unpack."

His wife touched his arm and smiled at Carlo.

"Is the small boy yours?" she asked.

"Oh, no, Signora. It was not a good idea." He watched her out of the corner of his eye as he picked up the bags. "One has, of course, too much of children at home."

They looked puzzled.

"Do you mean us?" she asked, and Carlo thought she glanced hurriedly at her husband. "Why did you happen to think we had children?"

"It was an accidental remark, Signora," said Carlo apologetically.

Signor Resta cleared his throat in rebuke and handed Carlo a room key.

"Number 410," he ordered, and to the Americans: "There is the telephone if one wishes anything. Or the porter will be of service in a clinch."

Twenty minutes later Carlo stood in front of the little cheese factory and faced a mathematical dilemma. Jacopo, according to his sisters, had left an hour ago; that meant he would have gone to the Hotel, which he hadn't, to Vittore's house, which was unlikely because of the distance, to Giorgio's cabanas or to Benozzo's restaurant. The dilemma was to make the right guess and avoid extra steps. There were, Carlo reasoned, so many minutes

111

in a day, so many feathers on a goose, and so many steps in a porter. Even an emergency could hardly be expected to change the laws of nature.

He chose Benozzo's, and as it happened, Jacopo at that very moment was seated at one of the outside tables, by the coffin-stone wall, helping Benozzo inscribe "Ristorante Benozzo" on the reverse side of forty picture post cards of Finale Ligure.

"It is an innovation suggested by Vittore," Benozzo explained. "I make a small profit on the sale of the post cards, and in addition advertise my restaurant."

Jacopo held up a picture of the square castelletto perched atop Crena Point. "It does not worry you that people might think this is your restaurant?"

Benozzo looked at the picture thoughtfully.

"Eigh," he said. "On that one write 'Ristorante Benozzo. No Climbing Necessary.'"

Jacopo lettered laboriously, spelling aloud as he formed the letters. He showed Benozzo the result.

"'Ristorante Benozzo,'" Benozzo read. "'No Americans Necessary.'" He paused and sighed, "Jacopo. We are not ourselves. We shall letter the post cards another day."

When Carlo came upon them they were watching the passing traffic, their elbows on the porcelain table top, their chins in their hands.

Benozzo raised his head and looked at him quizzically. "They have come?" he guessed.

"Wealthy," said Carlo. "And no children."

"It is . . . an answer to prayer," said Jacopo lugubriously.

"Vittore?" asked Carlo.

Benozzo spread his hands.

"He has gone to San Remo for the day. He heard of a farmer there who grew an olive with stripes like a gooseberry."

"A man of knowledge," said Jacopo, "must investigate these things."

Benozzo raised himself heavily from the table and bellowed toward the shadows behind him. "Tonio! Take care of the restaurant. I have business."

He jerked a large thumb in the general direction of Giorgio's cabana, and the three set off across the Piazza, led by the battle flag of Benozzo's mustache.

The canopied platform leading from the avenue to the beach shook under their three pairs of feet and startled Giorgio from his gloomy reverie into instant action.

"I am very busy!" he declared, seizing a wooden rake and skipping down the steps to the beach.

"I'll be spokesman," said Benozzo. "I understand Giorgio."

113

Jacopo mopped his face with a large handkerchief and nodded. Carlo shrugged. They followed Giorgio a few meters from the platform, where he was besieging a lone bottle cap with the rake.

"Very busy," he said again, alternately burying the bottle cap and unearthing it again.

"Giorgio," said Benozzo sternly. Jacopo quivered with admiration and suspense.

Giorgio cocked an eye at them and continued raking, until Benozzo planted himself in the way.

"My restaurant business will not wait until all the sand is off the beach," he said. "We must talk to you."

The rake came to a gradual halt, and the four of them stared at it in silence. Finally Giorgio moved, and Jacopo nudged Benozzo nervously.

Benozzo opened his mouth. "Carlo," he said, "has something to tell you."

The rake leaped and buried itself deep in the sand.

"I am very busy!" Giorgio shouted suddenly. "If you want to tell me the Americans have come, why don't you tell me the Americans have come? What is so much about the Americans coming? Americans have come before and Pepi is still here!" He gestured vaguely. "They probably have six children!"

"No children," said Carlo.

"And wealthy, Giorgio!" Benozzo added. "An auto-

114

mobile, Carlo says, like Signor Ghigliamo's parlor on wheels!"

"Seven pieces of luggage."

"And definitely no children. Carlo is certain!"

"Therefore, we must find Pepi and clean him up!"

Giorgio bridled.

"I keep him clean!" he said. "He may be a liar, and he may have an appetite like a puppy dog, but he is clean! If the Americans do not think he is clean enough, then there is no point in discussing it further!"

And he seized the rake again and set the sand to flying. For a long moment there were only the sounds of automobile horns on the town side, the shouts of children playing among the umbrellas on the beach and somewhere a discordant guitar.

Giorgio finished a furious path and straightened to survey his work.

"Are you still here?" he exclaimed in surprise.

Benozzo assumed an expression of pain. Carlo and Jacopo studied the sand at their feet.

"All right," said Giorgio with a sigh. "I suppose we must talk about it."

They adjourned to the cabana platform, arguing as they went. Benozzo felt that the success of Pepi's presentation depended on an artfully planned chance encounter. Carlo favored the more direct method of approaching the Americans at the Hotel. Jacopo of course agreed with both. Only Giorgio, knowing from the first he would be outvoted, insisted that nothing should be done without Vittore's sanction.

"Vittore would be disappointed in us," Benozzo argued, "if we had not at least decided on our method. And since Tonio will break every glass in my restaurant and eat all the salami if I don't get back soon, I suggest that we go there to plan the campaign."

Giorgio locked his cash register halfheartedly and lowered the wooden top of the ice chest. Very possibly, he thought, it would be no worse than usual. The American couple would give Pepi chewing gum, cluck over him like chickens with eggs to lay, rumple his hair—he could never keep Pepi's hair combed when Americans were around—and go away like all the others.

"Excuse me for mentioning it," said Jacopo, "but how can we present Pepi to the Americans when we don't have Pepi?"

Giorgio looked at him as if betrayed, then lifted the whistle that hung around his neck and blew a desultory peep.

"We may not see him for days," he prophesied hopefully. "There were some fishermen going out this morning, and he probably went with them."

But an answering trill came almost immediately, and

in a few seconds Pepi came bounding up the steps.

"Good morning!" he sang, hopping across the boards on one foot, being careful to miss the cracks. He teetered unsteadily and seized Giorgio's hand to right himself. Then, as he saw their faces, he put his other foot down quickly. "What have I done?"

"Nothing," Giorgio said shortly. "Once again you are going to be an American boy."

Pepi grinned with relief. "Yes, Giorgio."

"If you make a good impression," said Benozzo, "you will be very wealthy."

Jacopo nodded vigorously. "The American man is a ... a ..." He looked at Carlo appealingly.

"A—big shot," said Carlo, pantomiming a large cigar.

Giorgio drove his hands deep in his pockets, and Pepi promptly did likewise.

"You must be very polite," said Jacopo.

"I must smile at the lady," Pepi recited. "I must not swear."

"Go and put a shirt on," Giorgio ordered, "and some shoes. And meet us at Benozzo's."

"Shoes," repeated Pepi. He improvised quickly. "There was a wolf on the hill this morning—before you woke up, I mean. I threw my shoes at him, and he put them in his mouth and ran away!"

Giorgio grinned. His spirits were returning.

"What a liar, eh?" he asked proudly. Then to Pepi: "The wolf is an old friend of mine. He came back later and left your shoes."

"Okay," said Pepi in English, standing stiffly at attention. "Good morning. Good night. Got-a-match."

He clapped his hands and darted off. There was a brief pause.

"He's done it so many times," said Giorgio, "he thinks it's a game."

Chapter eight

Skirmish

Rοοм 410 overlooked the flat roof of the Hotel restaurant and the gleaming beach beyond. The shouts and laughter of the bathers came through a window that Harry Clune had opened almost as soon as the porter had left the room.

"Imagine keeping the blinds closed with that beautiful ocean to look at!" his wife had said.

They pretended that their faces were not damp from the unaccustomed heat. Expert by now at the art of packing and unpacking efficiently for short hotel visits, they had completed the necessary hanging, smoothing and straightening operations and were poring over a guidebook together.

"Grottoes," said Betty, tapping the page with a polished fingernail.

Harry grinned. "Sounds cool," he said.

"And tennis," she discovered with a laugh. *"That* sounds *hot!* Anyway, I like Italy. It's so . . . well, friendly."

"We certainly never got such attention anywhere else. Did you notice the porter? He never took his eyes off us."

Americans, they decided with tourists' characteristic logic, were an unusual spectacle. Harry consulted a scribbled note on the corner of a road map.

"Jacopo . . . Man-zo-ni," he recited carefully. "Or Manzoni Jacopo—they write their names backward here, you know. Shall we try to find him? Or take a walk first?"

"Oh, a walk first," she said eagerly. "I like to see something of a place first, with no one to explain. Just things. And people. I'd like to go back toward the middle of town where that big arch is. Do you remember it?"

He grunted good-naturedly. "Do I remember it! That was where the highway made a jog to the left and then to the right and suddenly it was like crossing Times Square against the traffic light!"

She shivered in mock terror. "I know. I shut my eyes."

He thrust the guidebook into his pocket and watched her as she fished for a lipstick in a new Parisian handbag. With her hand halfway to her mouth she stopped.

"Children," she said.

120

"Children?"

"The porter said something strange about children when we came in. What do you suppose he meant?"

"Your guess is as good as mine."

"It's odd," she mused, dropping her hand into her lap. "I'd been thinking about children all morning— ever since we crossed the border. All those . . . processions of orphans by the road."

He walked over and stood awkwardly beside her.

"Maybe they weren't orphans at all. Maybe they were . . . school children."

She shook her head. "Not at this time of year."

She began to apply her lipstick automatically, expertly, and spoke through lips drawn stiff for the process. "Orphan. Isn't it funny that there's a word for a child who lost its parents, but there's no word for parents who lost their child?"

There were several more or less direct ways to reach the Piazza XXV Aprile from the Hotel. There was the broad sandy Via Lido al Mare which led past the entrance to Giorgio's cabanas, the bicycle path, a small but shady promenade known rather elegantly as a park and the Via Aurelia itself, serving a dual purpose as a highway and arcaded business street. Therefore, in the normal course of events someone leaving Giorgio's cabanas for Benozzo's restaurant by any of these parallel

121

avenues would certainly arrive before two American turisti strolling aimlessly the entire distance from the Hotel.

But for Giorgio, Carlo, Benozzo and Jacopo the short route was not possible. First, because of Alfredo, who owned the cabanas adjoining Giorgio's. It was not that Alfredo was exactly dishonest, but operating cabanas is a business like any other, and if it becomes expedient during a rival neighbor's absence to sidle near his entrance and by means of discreet coughs, winks or beckoning gestures (which *could* be interpreted as idle passes at flies) encourage strangers to conclude that the main entrance is *this* way—well, who is to draw the thin dividing line between chicanery and mere acumen?

"It would not be kind of me," as Giorgio put it, "to tempt him."

Therefore the first leg of their course was a wide circle away from Alfredo's on which they narrowly missed actually encountering the Americans, who had stepped into a jewelry store.

The second detour was the result of a certain delicacy on Benozzo's part. There was, as it happened, another restaurant on the southeast corner of the Piazza whose outdoor portion projected across the end of the park. This establishment was managed by a Sicilian and exuded foreign smells to which Benozzo, as a Ligurian and restaurateur, was patriotically sensitive. To ignore their existence necessitated a solemn recrossing of the avenue, which was accomplished with dignity save for an unavailing groan from Carlo.

During the erratic circuit Giorgio found his thoughts to be of boyhood. Whether it was the remembered sight of Pepi scampering in the distance or the simple fact of having lived all his life in these surroundings, he could not have said. But the fine, modern bakery with a window full of loaves and macaroons and cassati reminded him of the huge community oven that once stood on the same site, and of his mother and the other women of the town who had brought their Christmas pandolce, fragrant with candied fruits and spices, and had gossiped gaily and endlessly throughout the baking.

The lofty bell tower of the Basilica, seen through a break in the buildings, enlivened many recollections. The long days of Lent, the traditional three-day silence of the bells, the Mass on the Saturday before Easter when the bright-eyed attentiveness of every boy was in reality secret expectancy—and the exultant dash across town, dodging bicycles, pedestrians and squealing automobiles, to the beach and thence, shouting happily, into the bracing water for the first official wading of the year.

There was the shop of Friedrich Theus, the Swiss watchmaker, who sat in his small window hour after hour peering at tiny parts through the protuberant lens which Giorgio, throughout his childhood, thought was some sort of deformity. Friedrich Theus, whose great age enabled him to remember the single time snow had magically appeared on the hillside, and all but the old and helpless had deserted the town and clambered breathlessly up the slopes to thrust their arms elbow-deep into the wondrous white stuff, throw handfuls of it into one another's delighted faces and even concoct from stolen sugar and lemons a kind of ice cream that excelled the delights of all ice cream before and since.

And there was Salvatore, the postman, a public servant even at the age of nine. At Christmastime he had helped Giorgio and the other children to compose their letters to Jesu Bambino and had come around on Epiphany Day to share the presents thus procured through his talents.

It had been a fine place for a boy, Giorgio thought. And one boyhood should be enough for any man. What pleasures there had been were simple and of the past and could surely not compare with the chromium-plated joys of the present and of America. But he wondered if the grape harvest in America meant for all the boys in town to don their bathing trunks and leap gleefully into the crushing. And if there were great empty buildings like the long-deserted prison on the hill where boys could race with echoes and other exciting terrors.

When they crossed the avenue for the last time and prepared to enter the Piazza from the south they would once again have met the American if old Ambruzzi the fisherman, mending his nets in front of Vicente's bath-house, hadn't had to enlist their aid. A donkey laden with basketed bottles of olive oil had mincingly sidestepped a trio of laughing girls in yellow shorts and was entangled in the nets. Somehow the combination of Jacopo's entreaties, Giorgio's strength, Benozzo's menacing mustache and the dolorous and therefore kindred expression on Carlo's face served to extricate him. But the incident had shattered Giorgio's reverie; the heavy redolence of olives brought to mind a grove high on the hill and a black-haired girl with laughter in her eyes and her skirt tucked above her knees.

As they passed under the Spanish Arch and stood waiting for the policeman on his pedestal to pit his shouts and gesticulations against the Piazza traffic, Giorgio felt himself very nearly as old as the street itself, which, except for the bakery, the new post office and the reconstructed Arch, had changed little during his lifetime.

"Three thousand years," said Harry Clune as he and his wife came through the arcade at the east end of the Piazza. "It was the Via Aurelia even in the days of the Roman conquests. Takes your breath away, doesn't it?"

She nodded. "I wonder if anyone ever thinks of that. I mean the people who live here all the time."

"I don't know. Pretty busy with the problems of to-day, I imagine."

He sighted his camera toward the bathhouse, where four men were using every means of cajolery to free a loaded donkey from the meshes of an old fisherman's net.

"One of them looks familiar," she said. "Like the porter at our hotel."

He laughed. "I suppose they all look as much alike to us as we do to them."

"I suppose so." She smiled, wondering ruefully if her smart seersucker suit and black blouse marked her merely as a visitor or as an ostentatious American sight-seer.

He took her elbow and grinned, reading her thoughts. "We *are* Americans," he said. "I don't think they'll mind as long as we don't chip pieces off the buildings for souvenirs."

They stopped halfway across the Piazza and craned their necks to read the inscription on the Arch.

"Hm," he grunted. "Rebuilt in 1937, as well as I can make out. It's probably the newest thing here—except for that post office we passed."

"Harry, look!" She swung him around by his arm. "That restaurant—with the outdoor tables and those queer-shaped stones at either end."

"Ris-to-ran-te Be-noz-zo," he read haltingly. "Maybe they have post cards."

The four card players in the rear of the restaurant glanced up briefly as they entered and returned to the

126

motionless scrutiny of their cards. Tonio, his Adam's apple betraying his panic, gripped the side of the counter and tried to remember some word in English. He had heard Americans say, "Non capisco," and consequently concluded that it was the same in both languages; otherwise he was helpless.

Harry's eyes lighted on the stack of post cards at the end of the counter. "Are these . . . for sale?" he asked, forming each syllable carefully.

Tonio stared at him in agony and tried shaking his head and nodding it at the same time, mumbling, "Non capisco."

"Oh," said Harry, replacing the cards. He turned to Betty. "Do you suppose I dare order a martini here?"

She laughed. "Remember what happened last time? In Ventimiglia?"

He grimaced. "I guess you're right. Vino might be safer."

Tonio's eyes brightened.

"Vino!" he said excitedly. "Vino. Vino. Vino rosso, vino bianco. Molto vino. Bellissimo vino!"

He motioned them to a table and began gathering bottles from the shelves in his long arms.

In the street Carlo stopped abruptly, and Jacopo stumbled into him.

"They're here!" said Carlo.

Giorgio took a step backward. "*Here!*" he echoed in dismay.

Benozzo snorted.

"And why not here?" he wanted to know. "My wine is good, my salami is as hard as a rock, my provolone——"

"Benozzo . . . I didn't mean that. I mean—it's only that we have no plan. . . !"

Giorgio started to turn away and gulped as he found himself gripped firmly by Jacopo, whose action was a nervous one, and Carlo, who had merely decided against a single farther step. The Americans had turned to look curiously at the tableau, and Giorgio felt the way he had many years ago when the photographer fastened a fearsome clamp to his head and made him stare unblinking at the baleful eye of the camera.

He smiled shakily, and Betty Clune smiled back at him.

"What a handsome man," she murmured to her husband.

Benozzo, suddenly aware of his duties, swept into the restaurant and relieved Tonio of his armful of wine bottles. With a flourish he deposited two glasses on the table and laid a bottle of the best wine against the flat of one huge hand.

"Bardolino?" he suggested.

"Why . . . yes, thanks. Er . . . grazie," said Harry. He glanced uncertainly toward Giorgio, who was still imprisoned between Carlo and Jacopo.

"Do you suppose he's in some kind of trouble?" he

128

whispered to Betty. "He doesn't seem to be very happy."

"No trouble," said Benozzo in English. "Scusate . . . excuse, please. I do not mean to interrupt, but there is no trouble."

Harry grinned with relief. "I'm glad somebody speaks English."

Benozzo beamed and motioned the others to come closer. The card players, sensing a diversion, put down their cards and turned to watch.

"My English," said Benozzo, "is not very good. But my friend Giorgio . . ." Giorgio struggled fruitlessly and surrendered, letting himself be propelled to the table. "Giorgio speaks English like an American."

Harry rose and extended his hand. "How do you do?" he said. "My name is Clune—Harry Clune. And this is my wife, Mr. . . . ?"

"Cappelletti," said Giorgio, trapped. "Giorgio Cappelletti."

"Will you . . . have a glass of wine with us?"

The "No, grazie—thank you . . ." that came to his lips was his own, but the contradictory action of sitting abruptly was engineered by the forces behind him. He swallowed helplessly.

"Thank you," he repeated.

"These also," said Benozzo expansively, pouring three glasses of wine, "are my friends, Carlo Piemonte and Jacopo Manzoni."

"Manzoni!" Betty exclaimed.

129

Harry was on his feet, pumping Jacopo's hand.

"This is really a surprise!" he said. "I guess you wouldn't believe this, but we know a very good friend of yours. In fact he told us to look you up."

Jacopo's head bobbed happily.

"Scusate," said Benozzo. "He knows of your friend, but he does not speak English."

"Grazie," said Jacobo, beaming. "Molti grazie."

"But Giorgio," Benozzo bellowed over the ensuing laughter, handshaking and pouring of two more glasses of wine, "is the best interpreter this side of Genoa!"

Giorgio would happily have disclaimed the designation and in fact imperiled it by speaking haltingly in English to Jacopo and directing a flow of Italian to the Americans. In the hilarity which followed he reddened, bolted his wine and stood up.

"I must go," he said in English. "There is no one at the cabana!"

In his haste to escape Benozzo's restraining hands he nearly collided with Pepi, who chose that moment to trot in clumsily in unaccustomed shoes.

"Go!" Giorgio said hoarsely, pushing the boy with both hands. "Go get dressed."

"I am dressed!" replied Pepi, aggrieved.

Betty Clune smiled. "What a perfectly beautiful child!" she said. "Is he yours?"

"Go! I am talking business!" Giorgio whispered, but

Benozzo had seized Pepi's shoulders and was steering him toward the Americans.

"He is nobody's," said Benozzo tragically. "He has no parents. No family. It is very sad."

"Oh, dear!" said Betty.

Her husband frowned. "That's—a shame," he said.

Pepi squirmed under Benozzo's heavy hand, remembered to smile shyly at the lady and tried to dig a hole in the floor with his toe.

"Giorgio tries to take care of him," Benozzo explained in a tone whose mournfulness implied that no little boy could survive such care. "But . . ." He shrugged his shoulders eloquently.

Giorgio was alarmed to notice that the Americans exchanged a serious glance.

Harry Clune stood up. "If you can't stay with us now, Mr. Cappelletti," he said, "perhaps you and Mr. Manzoni can join us tonight for dinner at the Hotel."

Although the words "at the Hotel" grieved Benozzo, he suppressed his feelings bravely and released Pepi long enough to stroke his mustache in an unmistakable signal.

"Dinner?" said Giorgio, whose command of English seemed to have forsaken him.

Harry smiled. "We can't very well talk without you, can we?"

Carlo translated for Jacopo, who nodded vigorously.

131

Giorgio, his heart in his throat as Betty Clune reached toward Pepi's curls, stammered acceptance.

Giorgio the scholar, he thought later as he strode angrily toward the cabanas with Pepi at his heels. This is what happens when you let yourself learn a foreign language!

Chapter nine

Assault

ALESSANDRO the cat lay on the cool marble top of Giorgio's old dresser and recalled with lazy satisfaction the recent stalking of a butterfly. The turmoil that filled the three small rooms of his master's house with noise and confusion seemed to him as clumsy as all other human enterprises. If the large creature with the tremendous whiskers and the little round creature with the very damp face truly wanted to capture Giorgio, they should crouch silently until he stopped moving and then pounce on him. Instead they followed him from room to room, side-stepping chairs, rounding tables, dodging the slanting overhead beams—and always having to step over the legs of the fourth creature, who sat dolefully on the edge of the bed.

Their weapons, too, Alessandro considered pitifully inadequate. One of them brandished a white shirt, and the other waved a long colored flag of some sort whose very combination of hues would frighten away a nervous prey.

"It is an excellent tie," the larger of the two stalkers was insisting. "It was sent to me from Rome by my brother Mario."

Giorgio nimbly skirted the rocking chair and pushed it in the way of his pursuers.

"I don't want to wear it," he said, and then added hurriedly, "I mean because of the . . . the responsibility, Benozzo."

"It didn't cost my brother anything," Benozzo assured him, reaching forward in a futile attempt to drape it around Giorgio's neck. "It was given to him in payment of a bet. Something to do with horses."

Giorgio, still edging away, eyed the necktie dubiously. "Without a doubt," he said.

Carlo pulled his feet out of the way for the seventh or eighth time and observed from the edge of the bed, "Giorgio is not concerned with the bets your brother Mario lost. But the shirt—Giorgio, why won't you compromise? At least wear the white shirt."

Giorgio stopped, and Jacopo gasped with relief and handed him the shirt.

"Jacopo isn't wearing a white shirt," Giorgio argued.

"I don't *have* a white shirt," said Jacopo plaintively.

"The shoes," Benozzo pronounced. "Carlo, they should shine like mirrors. I am told Americans look first at the shoes."

Carlo obediently bent to pull the shoes from Giorgio's reluctant feet.

"If they look at my shoes," Giorgio reasoned, "why must I wear a white shirt?"

But he knew the opportunity for effective resistance had passed. And Alessandro, seeing that the chase was over, went to sleep.

"Shoes! Shirts! Neckties from Rome!" grumbled Giorgio. "We should have waited for Vittore!"

Benozzo sighed grandly. "What can a wise man do," he wanted to know, "that we clever men have not already done?"

"Giorgio," said Jacopo timidly, "one would think you are opposed to the idea!"

"Of course he isn't," said Benozzo, struggling to remove Giorgio's shirt. "Giorgio is only careful. He knows an idea is like a fox. It tries to get away from you—or to bite you. An idea must be handled carefully."

"This idea," Carlo pointed out dryly, "is a fox which has been with us for a year. It has had time to become tame."

Benozzo lifted the shirt aloft triumphantly and dropped it on the floor.

"Besides, Giorgio," he said, "Carlo and I will be on hand to help. And Vittore, too, if he comes back in time. We," he declared, "will have dinner tonight at the adjoining table. And if you need help . . ."

He gestured broadly with the other shirt.

"You will be the general," Jacopo told Giorgio, "I shall be the adjutant, and Benozzo and Carlo will be the flanking army."

Carlo breathed on one of the shoes and buffed it energetically on his sleeve.

"What *is* in your mind, Giorgio?" he asked. "What are you thinking?"

Giorgio didn't answer. He brushed Alessandro off the dresser top and leaned down to look in the mirror, fumbling with the buttons of his shirt. His father and mother looked at him sternly and out of the unchangeable past, from a small leather double frame. From a larger frame of hand-carved chestnut, Maria gazed at him with a half-smile that for the first time seemed mocking. And from the mirror itself a face frowned at him ferociously.

"I'll tell you the truth," he said at last, turning around and stepping over Alessandro. "I don't know what I'm thinking."

The sunset was commonplace, which is to say that it was of a routine magnificence, the kind Ligurians apologize for the way people elsewhere apologize for bad weather. It bathed the windows of the church and the cheese factory with equal radiance and made the Spanish Arch no more richly golden than it made an overturned wooden hurdle left on the beach by a diverted athlete. In its catholic glow even Giorgio's face shone deceptively as the four men stopped in the middle of the Piazza.

"It's too early," Giorgio said hopefully.

"Any successful campaign," Benozzo contradicted, "depends on the surprise element."

"What is the surprise?" Giorgio argued. "Jacopo and I are invited!"

"The surprise," offered Carlo, "will be the necktie."

Benozzo glowered at him and barely restrained Giorgio from removing it at once.

"It's very pretty," said Jacopo comfortingly. "And of course it will improve somewhat after dark."

Benozzo gestured impatiently. "The plan," he said. "You and Jacopo will meet the Americans in the Hotel dining room. Pepi will be there as soon as he closes the cabana."

"I ought to help him," Giorgio began. "He may forget to see that the bathhouses are locked——"

Benozzo took his arm firmly.

"If *I* am willing," he said, "to leave the fortunes of my restaurant in the hands of a donkey like Tonio, you can make the small sacrifice of forgetting the bath-houses!"

"We are all making sacrifices," Carlo pointed out. "If I am seen eating in the Hotel dining room I may be discharged."

"Why?" asked Giorgio. "It's your night off."

"Exactly," said Carlo mournfully. "Signor Resta will suspect me of having become mentally unbalanced."

"Come," Benozzo ordered. "It's time to go. Giorgio, you and Jacopo go first. Carlo and I will follow you later and take the nearest table in the dining room. If you need any help in persuading them to adopt Pepi——"

"Please!" Giorgio interrupted. "If you help me much more you'll have them adopting *me!* Come, Jacopo."

Benozzo watched them go toward the Hotel with a slight frown.

"I would feel much easier," he said to Carlo, "if Vittore were here."

Carlo nodded. Vittore was a man versed not only in ideas but in all the antecedents of each idea. He was a man who, by his own admission, fashioned ideas out of the clay of facts and polished them with logic. A campaign without Vittore might conceivably succeed by a haphazard chain of circumstances, but a campaign with Vittore would be classically symmetrical even in failure.

Benozzo having decided that the solace of a cigar

would compensate somewhat for Vittore's absence, they walked slowly back across the Piazza toward the restaurant, circling a parked bus in which a group of English schoolgirls waited for their mistress to find her place in the guidebook.

"Finale Ligure," she stated. "Famous for . . . famous for . . ."

She snapped the book shut in frustration and peered at the Arch.

". . . for its beautiful Arch," she continued, as every eye but hers veered hypnotically to the largest mustache they had ever seen.

"And—" she saw the corner of the park ahead— "for its luxuriant vegetation."

Hours later in her hotel room in Genoa she was to lie awake pondering the mysterious forces that would send an entire busload of proper young ladies into abrupt and uncontrollable hysteria.

"Bottled water," she would conclude, "and too much seasoning in the food."

Outside the restaurant Benozzo came to a sudden halt. "Vittore!" he exclaimed.

Vittore got up from the table and walked out to meet him.

"Vittore! You came back!"

"The olive," Vittore explained, "had been accidentally eaten by a sailor. I suspect it was a fraud anyway.

I have had some experience with husbandry and——"

Benozzo waved the subject aside with a temerity born of urgency. He quickly summarized the events of the day.

"All the sense seems to have left Giorgio's head," he grieved. "We do not know what has replaced it. *He* doesn't know what has replaced it!"

Carlo nodded. "He admits he doesn't know."

Vittore considered for a moment.

"His wits will sharpen in the conflict," he decided. "In such a delicate engagement, it is often the way. Naturally I will take charge."

Gino, the waiter, counted his time in the Hotel dining room worth while only when an absence of customers enabled him to linger on the open veranda side and look longingly at the beach. He left his point of vantage with a mutter of resignation when a party of four appeared in the doorway. After all, he told himself, it was getting dark, and two of the party were Americans, which was another way of saying there would be a substantial tip.

Halfway to the door he began bowing and then straightened suddenly as he recognized Giorgio and Jacopo. "Good evening," he said, addressing himself directly to Giorgio's necktie.

"It came from Rome," said Giorgio with some truculence. "A table for four, please."

"It was probably exiled," murmured Gino. "This way, please." He led the way to a table on the veranda.

Giorgio hesitated.

"The tables are too close together," he complained.

Gino closed his eyes and silently bemoaned his role. "I assumed," he said coldly, "that all of the party intended to sit at the same table."

"What's he saying?" Harry Clune wanted to know.

"He . . . asks if the table is all right," Giorgio said in English.

Harry grinned at Gino. "Sure. It's fine. Er . . . buono."

Gino, vindicated, bowed and held a chair for Betty Clune.

"What a lovely view!" she said as she sat down.

Gino looked at her blankly.

"She says," said Giorgio in Italian, "that the view is pretty enough to make up for the service."

Gino's eyebrows expressed acute pain.

"Jacopo," he pleaded, "this is to be a short meal, no? Perhaps just some cheese and a little wine?"

He stalked off in search of menus.

Jacopo smiled uncertainly at the Clunes. "Giorgio," he suggested, "hadn't you better say something for me?"

Giorgio translated freely. "Jacopo says he . . . hopes you will enjoy your dinner."

"I'm sure we will," said Harry heartily. "Buono."

"Buono," Giorgio repeated for Jacopo's benefit.

"I understand that," said Jacopo, somewhat pained, "but what did *I* say?"

Giorgio, who was facing the door, started up out of

his chair. "Vittore!" he exclaimed. He turned to Betty. "Excuse me. It is a friend of mine. If you would excuse me . . . ?"

In his excitement at seeing a flanking army of three instead of two, he hurried halfway across the dining room before realizing he had spoken in Italian. He looked back, worried, and was relieved to see that Jacopo and Harry were beaming at each other and exchanging buonos.

"Vittore," Giorgio whispered, "what am I supposed to do!"

"First," said Vittore calmly, as Benozzo and Carlo waited, "let us examine the facts."

"Yes."

"The facts are these. The Americans are wealthy. They are interested in children."

"Well . . ."

"These are the facts. They are interested in children. Pepi is a child. They are, therefore, interested in Pepi."

"I don't . . . know," said Giorgio. "There has been no discussion."

Vittore spread his hands. "That is why we are here: to see that the discussion can be conducted without distraction."

"What distraction?"

Vittore looked at him keenly. "Did you talk to Maria?"

Giorgio paused, then nodded his head unhappily.

"There then! It is settled. Pepi must be adopted. It is as we have always said: a small boy is a nuisance unless one has money."

Giorgio stiffened. "Pepi is not exactly a nuisance."

"*All* small boys are nuisances, unless their parents have money." Vittore tapped himself on the chest. "I was a nuisance to my parents when I was a small boy."

"Besides," Benozzo interpolated in a hoarse whisper, "we must think of Pepi."

"No distractions," commanded Vittore. "If you need us——"

"I know, I know!" said Giorgio. "You will help."

When Gino returned with four menus he found Vittore, Benozzo and Carlo seated at the adjacent table, bowing and smiling at the Clunes.

"Very friendly people," said Harry.

"They certainly are," Betty agreed. "I've never seen anything quite like it."

"Frankly, Mr. Cappelletti, my wife and I had no idea the Italians were so friendly."

Giorgio's pride momentarily overcame his discomfort.

"We are Ligurians, Signore. Liguria is a friendly country."

Betty looked surprised. "Country? Isn't it part of Italy?"

Giorgio shrugged.

"Italy is many countries, Signora. The Umbrians are smart, the Pisans like to work hard, the Ligurians are friendly. . . ."

Gino thrust the menus belligerently on the table.

Harry glanced at one doubtfully. "We're going to have to put ourselves in your hands at this point. What should we order?"

Feeling a surreptitious tug at his trousers, Giorgio started to translate for Jacopo and quailed as he met Gino's cold eye.

"Gino," he said desperately, "we shall have a truce. The service is superior. Listen—I'll tell them so."

Gino melted perceptibly. "A truce," he agreed. "The necktie is beautiful. You see, we are friends again. We even lie for each other."

On the beach, couples were begining to drift to a large platform erected for dancing. A violin and two accordions struck up an American tune.

"In our honor." Harry smiled.

"I . . . I don't think so," said Giorgio, wondering if he was being impolite. "It is a dance for the people who work at the seaplane factory. It will be difficult to talk," he added, "with the music."

"Not at all," said Betty. "It makes everything even nicer."

Harry settled comfortably in his chair. "The music

144

does make it nicer," he said. "Makes it seem like a special occasion, doesn't it?"

Giorgio surveyed his area of operation. Jacopo, perched nervously on the edge of his chair awaiting another opportunity to say buono. Vittore, Benozzo and Carlo, their elbows on the table, ignoring him with elaborate care. Gino, waiting with pencil poised and the face of a fisherman with an empty boat.

"A special occasion," Giorgio said miserably.

His back was turned toward the beach, or he also would have seen Maria, in her best peach-colored dress, mounting the dancing platform with Ricardo, the handsome line foreman from the seaplane factory.

Chapter ten

The Flanking Army

THE ears of d'Annunzio!" exclaimed Sergio, the cook. He loved to swear, and his highly personal and anatomical brand of profanity filled the kitchen with a rich assortment of imaginary celebrities of all eras, or at least with portions of them.

"The legs and arms of Lorenzo!" he said cheerfully. "The finger tips of a snake!" He was frequently more eloquent than literal.

He was not the kind of cook who supervised with lordly aloofness, sniffing here and lifting a lid there. Sergio preferred being in every pot, bin and bowl up to his elbows. He was everywhere in the kitchen at once, chopping, slicing, stirring, tasting, dredging and swearing.

"Destruction!" he bawled as he thrust a lazy butcher boy aside and wielded the cleaver with his own brawny, flour-covered arm. It was his favorite epithet. It may indeed have been his entire philosophy. Certainly there was lusty fervor in the way he smashed the smug perfection of an egg or twisted a clove of garlic from the accustomed security of its stem. Even the heavy black letters on his daily order lists he seemed to grind into the pristine note pages with the air of a conqueror. One would suspect that the act of plunging a defenseless handful of linguine into boiling water or a half-dozen plum tomatoes into a pan of spitting, popping oil gave him more satisfaction than the resulting creation.

His complaints were continuous, titanic and good-natured. He castigated the heat of the stove, the coldness of the refrigerator, the slowness of the waiters, the speed of the orders, the length of the serving table, the shortness of pot handles and now the strains of music that began to float in from the twilit beach.

"Music!" he roared. Music meant dancing, and dancing meant hungry couples wandering in for food long after the kitchen would be closed. "The teeth of Puccini!"

He trimmed a knuckle of veal with expert strokes and strode to the dining-room door, swinging the cleaver as he went, while the butcher boy, the dishwasher, the baker and Gino's fellow waiter fled from his path.

147

Adjusting his eye to the little diamond-shaped window in the door, he glared into the other world of idle diners who were oblivious of the trials and crises of culinary administration. The cleaver stopped in mid-air.

"Carlo!" he exclaimed. "Giorgio! Vittore! Jacopo! *Benozzo!*"

"He must have cut himself," the dishwasher whispered. "His swearing has a note of reality!"

"The leisure classes are bad enough," rumbled Sergio, the leisure classes to his way of thinking consisting of all persons who ate while he worked, "but tonight we serve spies as well! Even little ones under the age limit for spying!"

This last was in reference to Pepi, who had trotted across the veranda from the beach and drawn himself up on a chair at the side of the dining room.

"Isn't that your little boy?" Betty Clune asked Giorgio.

"Si," he said. "Yes, that is Pepi."

"Couldn't he have dinner with us?"

Giorgio was shocked. "Oh, no, Signora! He eats like a puppy dog!"

To demonstrate he tossed Pepi a bread stick from the basket Gino had put on the table. Pepi caught it, wriggled contentedly and consumed it in three almost instantaneous bites. Giorgio felt better, but only for a moment.

148

"Isn't he adorable, Harry?" he heard Betty murmur.

He felt rather than heard a stirring at the next table and was suddenly engrossed in the menu.

"Prosciutto," he said abruptly. "You like prosciutto?"

Jacopo sighed happily.

"Pro . . . ?" Harry ventured.

"Oh, scusate . . . excuse me. It is ham. Very good. With melon."

"That sounds wonderful," said Betty.

Giorgio relayed the order to Gino, who translated it into an illegible scrawl on his pad.

"How old is he?" Betty asked.

Giorgio found the menu suddenly fascinating.

"Spaghetti marinara," he read loudly, "spaghetti al pesto, spaghetti carbonera, spaghetti con olio e aglio, spaghetti con funghi, spaghetti con salsa di carne. You like spaghetti?"

"Sure," said Harry. He laughed. "Back home we just order Italian spaghetti and let it go at that!"

"How old did you say the boy is?" asked Betty.

Giorgio sighed. "Six," he said, his face eloquently apologetic. A hopeless age, the very worst of ages, an age to make one ashamed. He repeated sepulchrally, "Six."

"That's a fine age," said Betty. "I think it's one of the nicest ages of all, don't you?"

Gino, his pencil wavering over his pad, looked at Jacopo doubtfully.

149

"What kind of spaghetti," he asked, "do you think they are talking about?"

With a show of immediate contrition, Giorgio resumed his cataloguing of spaghetti styles.

It was, of course, Vittore, glancing toward the beach, who saw Maria first.

"An unfortunate coincidence," he muttered to Benozzo. "Ricardo is not a favorite rival."

They watched the dancing for a moment in silence. Ricardo was a head taller than most of the other men, a head gleaming with straight, black hair, reflected like a helmet in the lantern light.

"If he knows Giorgio is in the neighborhood," Carlo observed, "his head is as smooth inside as it is outside."

Benozzo stroked his mustache for inspiration.

"It seems to me," he volunteered, "that this is a good thing. It may bring Giorgio to his senses."

Vittore looked at Giorgio's unsuspecting back.

"No," he said thoughtfully. "We must protect him. Not from Ricardo but from the distraction. We must keep him from looking toward the beach."

Gino drew an important-looking squiggle on his pad representing spaghetti al pesto and placed a 4 in front of it.

Harry cleared his throat. "About that boy of yours, Mr. Cappelletti . . . " he began.

"And wine!" said Giorgio explosively. "We must

150

have wine! What am I thinking of! There is Chianti, Bardolino, Lambrusco, Orvieto, Soave . . . "

"Whatever you say," Harry agreed, somewhat startled. Darned friendly people, he said to himself. Darned friendly.

Giorgio succeeded in occupying the first two courses with a lengthy description of the cabana business, winegrowing, squid fishing, iron mining and Liguria. Twice he turned to point down the beach toward Caprazoppa, and twice he found Benozzo standing breathlessly in the way, explaining that he had dropped his fork.

"Is it necessary," Jocopo asked plaintively the second time, rubbing his elbow, "to drop it with such force and so far from your own table?"

"Some restaurants," replied Benozzo with dignity, "provide forks with firmer handles."

Harry finished the last of his spaghetti and turned to Giorgio. "As we were saying about the boy, Mr. Cappelletti——"

"You like the spaghetti?" asked Giorgio urgently.

"Why . . . yes, it was fine."

"Delicious," said Betty.

"Good!" Giorgio signaled Gino frantically. "It is very special, the way spaghetti is cooked only here and in Genova—Genoa. You sure you like it?"

"Very much," Harry insisted.

"Gino! Ancora spaghetti."

Betty started. "Oh dear, if that means more . . ."

Harry coughed. "Er . . . dear," he said, "when in Liguria . . . you know . . . "

She sank back in her chair and smiled weakly at Giorgio.

"What's the matter with him?" whispered Benozzo hoarsely at the next table.

Vittore pulled his ear. "The spaghetti is not that good," he observed.

"It is terrible!" exclaimed Benozzo, who had eaten every morsel. "They should be eating *my* spaghetti al pesto!"

The meat course was scallopine alla Marsala. Giorgio, during a detailed account of last summer's swimming race across the Gulf, filled a small extra plate and signaled Gino to give it to Pepi.

Betty watched with interest and suddenly interrupted Giorgio's narrative. "Excuse me," she said. "But is that *wine* he's being given?"

Giorgio glanced at her in surprise. "He gets dry from so many bread sticks."

"But—wine. I mean . . . he's such a little boy."

Giorgio's face cleared. "I understand, Signora," he said. "But we don't give him the *good* wine."

"I see," said Betty, choking a little.

"Mr. Cappelletti," said Harry purposefully, "while we're speaking of Pepi——"

Giorgio patted himself on the stomach and forced a wide smile. "The scallopine—it is good, eh?"

They nodded.

"Wonderful," said Betty.

"Gino!" Giorgio ordered. "Ancora scallopine!"

There was a strained silence, until Jacopo hitched himself forward in his chair.

"Giorgio," he begged, "say something for me again."

Giorgio looked at him bleakly, noticed that Betty's eyes were once again on Pepi and drew a deep breath.

"Jacopo," he said, "wants to know all about America."

Harry smiled. "*All* about America is a pretty big order," he said, "but we'll do our best."

Baseball, New York City and American automotive engineering carried them through the second serving of scallopine and generous bowls of ice cream.

"It's a good place," Harry said, "for kids. You know —youngsters."

Giorgio raised his hand for Gino and signaled toward his ice cream. "Gino," he said hoarsely.

"Please," Betty protested. "No!"

Giorgio assumed an expression of astonishment. "You don't like ice cream!" he exclaimed.

"Oh, yes. It was delicious, but . . . "

He brightened. "You would rather have fruit!" he said. "Gino——"

Harry tugged at his collar. "Uh . . . Mr. Cappelletti . . ."

Giorgio clapped his hand to his forehead. "Stupido!" he cried. "We will have both!"

Jacopo closed his eyes with sheer joy. At the flanking table Benozzo made involuntary chopping gestures with one huge hand, and Vittore shook his head slowly.

Struck with a sudden thought in the middle of his ice cream with figs and peaches, Jacopo stopped with loaded spoon upraised.

"Giorgio," he said, "what did they say about Pepi?"

Giorgio racked his brain for the words of the dance music being played and began to sing lustily.

"It is a good tune, no?" he asked eagerly.

But the name "Pepi" had done the damage. This time Harry was not to be thwarted.

"Mr. Cappelletti," he said, "my wife and I want to talk to you if you can spare us a little time."

Giorgio nodded, his resourcefulness at an ebb. Above the noise of music and laughter on the beach, he imagined he heard Maria's voice, singing the same song he had tried to remember. He turned to look just as Benozzo's ice-cream dish skidded across the floor.

"It's all right," Benozzo assured them, maneuvering the dish back and forth behind Giorgio's chair with his foot. "It was empty. Please, Giorgio, don't bother to help me. You mustn't turn your back on your guests."

"Perhaps," Harry suggested, "we could go up to our room and talk. It seems . . . rather busy down here."

Giorgio sank lower into his chair. "I don't speak English very well," he said.

Betty was surprised.

"Nonsense!" she said. "You speak it beautifully."

"Thank you, Signora. But . . . I have used up all I know!"

There was a distinct cough from the next table and the scrape of a chair.

"Scusi, Signore, Signora," said Vittore with a courtly bow and a cold look at Giorgio. "Giorgio is worried about Pepi's bedtime."

Giorgio, stunned by the support from an unexpected quarter, could only repeat, "Si. Pepi's bedtime."

"Therefore," said Vittore smoothly, "*I* will see that Pepi goes to bed, and you may be with your friends."

Harry beamed. "Well, that's mighty fine of you!" he exclaimed, taking a handful of cigars from his pocket, at which Benozzo instantly joined them.

Giorgio, a cigar unnaturally between his teeth, found his wits. Pepi's bedtime was an hour away.

"But Pepi won't go to bed for——" he began.

"Jacopo will help me," Vittore interrupted pointedly. He smiled at Harry and Betty. "In matters concerning Pepi," he said, "Giorgio is very careful. Sometimes," he added in Italian to Giorgio, "so careful that, like a

155

cautious fisherman, he misses the opportunity for a big catch."

Again he bowed, and over his head Giorgio caught a brief glimpse of the dancers on the beach. That big conceited Ricardo, he thought—it's a good thing he doesn't know Maria is free tonight or he wouldn't be wasting his time at a company dance. He'd be standing on her doorstep, begging her—with lies, of course—to stop waiting for that no-good Giorgio.

In the kitchen Sergio wiped his hands on his apron and glared suspiciously at Gino.

"Who paid for the dinner?" he asked.

Gino shrugged. "The American," he said. "And Vittore for the other table."

"And the tip?"

"Very small," Gino lied, keeping a tight grip on the wad of lire in his pocket. "Americans, too. It is surprising."

"No matter," Sergio decided. "I outwitted Benozzo!"

"How?"

"He'll never bring his spies here again! The elbows of Dante!" He exulted. "He was beside himself. I saw him throwing things on the floor in rage!"

"But how did you outwit him?"

"I used his own recipe for the pesto!"

Chapter eleven

Night Music

It WAS an excellent cigar, Giorgio knew, and the fault was his rather than its if it gave him so little of the solace most cigar smokers seemed to derive. He wished he were not ignorant of the mysteries so clearly mastered by men like Benozzo and Vittore, who were able to sense an answer by thoughtfully rolling a cigar between the fingers, or see a conclusion by peering meditatively into its glowing end. The very ritual of applying a match, whether in a rushing blaze from one of Benozzo's sulphurous torches or the quiet, chaste flame into which Vittore delicately introduced a cigar tip, held secrets for the initiated only. The fact that Benozzo indulged continually and with great billows of smoke, while Vittore's one cigar a day emitted only the gentlest wisp of vapor, Giorgio attributed to Vittore's intellectual superiority. Obviously a man of vast knowledge required less inspiration.

As for himself, he felt that he never had greater need of whatever mystic key existed; yet try as he might, he could extract nothing from his cigar but a slight giddiness. Standing glumly at the window of the Clunes' hotel room while Harry arranged chairs and Betty emptied ash trays, he tried to recall the cigar-smoking vocabulary with which his friends seemed able to hold one another, at least temporarily, at bay.

"It seems to me . . ." followed by a long pause and inhalation, demanded a respectful silence from one's fellow smoker. A wave of the cigar and a disdainful ejection of smoke from the nostrils, at least when practiced by Vittore, reduced the other's arguments to nothing. And there was "Eh, now . . . !" accompanied by a direct pointing of the cigar as if it were a weapon, which was as much as saying, "Now I have you! With your own statement you have walked right into my trap!"

"There," said Betty. "Now I think we can be comfortable."

They seated themselves, and Giorgio was disheartened to see that Harry, smoking easily and with evident pleasure, had nearly finished his cigar. He was obviously of the fraternity.

"Now then," said Harry. "I'll be perfectly frank with you, Mr. Cappelletti. I . . . don't want to say anything wrong. In fact, I hope you'll stop me if I do, but—" he looked at the glowing tip of his cigar—"it's about your boy, Pepi. My wife has taken quite a liking to him."

Giorgio nodded dumbly.

Betty leaned forward, her eyes anxious. "Please tell us if we're saying something we shouldn't," she begged. "But . . . you did say the boy had no parents."

"In other words," Harry said, "you're not his official guardian. Is that right?"

"Guardian?" Giorgio repeated, blinking smoke from his eyes.

"I mean—are you the boy's foster father? Have you ever adopted him?"

Giorgio hesitated, then shook his head honestly. He heard a little gasp of relief, and Betty put her hand on her husband's arm. "What did I tell you, Harry? It was providence!"

She seemed to moisten her lips. "Mr. Cappelletti, would you consider letting someone else adopt Pepi?"

The smoke in Giorgio's eyes stung remarkably. "Adopt . . ." he said foolishly.

Harry cleared his throat and stood up. "We're probably going about this all wrong," he said.

Giorgio stared hard at his cigar.

"It seems to me . . ." he began. They waited while he inhaled deeply and blew the smoke toward the ceiling.

"Yes?" said Betty finally.

"You were saying it seemed to you . . ." reminded Harry.

Giorgio felt a cough starting in his throat and swallowed hard. "I have forgotten," he said.

Betty's voice began again, very softly, so softly that he had to strain to hear above the ringing in his ears.

"You see, Mr. Cappelletti, we lost our own little boy some time ago."

Giorgio was genuinely shocked. "You *lost* him!" he exclaimed.

Harry walked behind his wife's chair and put his hands on her shoulders.

"My wife means he died," he said quietly.

It seemed to Giorgio that even the eddies of smoke in the room shivered and stood still. The ringing in his ears increased from piercing embarrassment. Gradually he became aware of Betty sitting opposite him and Harry standing silently behind her and of the distant music from the beach.

He hit his forehead with his fist. "I am a big fool!" he groaned.

Betty smiled. "Of course you're not."

Giorgio noticed a frayed place in the rug in front of him. He covered it slowly with his foot.

"I am sorry," he said. "It is a hard thing to . . . lose someone you love." Then, lest they read his thoughts, he added quickly, "I remember when my mother died,

160

and my father two years later. Of course, that was a long time ago. I was nineteen."

"Our little boy would have been just about Pepi's age by now," Betty told him. "This is . . . something we've often talked about. But in America adoption often takes a long, long time. And we heard there were so many . . . orphans in Italy. We are planning to go to the authorities in one of the cities. You see, we thought we could help one of them and at the same time . . ."

She stopped and turned to Harry for help. He coughed.

"If we're out of line, Mr. Cappelletti . . ." he began.

Giorgio looked up. "Line?" he asked. "I do not know this—'out of line.'"

"What I'm trying to say is, if there's something wrong with the idea . . ."

Giorgio put down his cigar and rubbed the knuckles of one hand.

"Pepi—doesn't speak much English," he stammered.

Betty's peal of relieved laughter startled him. "Is that all?" she cried.

Giorgio permitted himself a wan smile. He drew back his feet as Harry walked in front of him to the window.

"There is a hole in the rug," he explained apologetically.

The three of them studied the hole for a long moment, until Harry broke the silence.

"I think we ought to tell you something about ourselves," he said.

Giorgio listened in partial embarrassment and partial wonder to the details of the Clunes' daily life. One already knew, of course, that all houses in America were like small hotels, with hot water for washing and cold water for drinking at any time of day or night. And that there were great numbers of bathrooms, all indoors. And that little boys had huge rooms to themselves and played endlessly with electric trains as big as bicycles.

The houses stood apart, too, like villas, and people lived in one city and worked in another, all owning large automobiles, yet traveling many hours every day on trains. These things had puzzled him before, and he was further bemused by the thought of Pepi returning someday to explain the many mysteries of American life. Pepi, sitting in Benozzo's restaurant telling wonderful stories with a grownup's deep voice, and staring with tolerant amusement at the funny little town of his boyhood. Would he be pale like an American, and would he look with secret laughter on the dark, simple faces of old Benozzo and old Jacopo and old Carlo and old Giorgio and very, very old Vittore? Or would he come back at all?

Harry Clune, still standing beside the window, had stopped speaking.

"I'm sorry," said Giorgio. "I was thinking."

Dance music still drifted in through the window, and Betty's soft voice could barely be heard over it.

"Harry," she said. "I think Mr. Cappelletti would like more time."

Harry turned from the window. "Sure," he said anxiously. "We don't want to hurry you. I suppose this is—kind of sudden."

"We'll understand perfectly if you'd rather not answer right now."

"Tell you what," suggested Harry, "why don't you sleep on it?" Then, seeing Giorgio's brow start to furrow: "That is—think it over and meet us here for breakfast."

He fumbled in his pocket and drew out a fresh cigar.

"Would you like another?" he asked, nodding toward the half-finished cigar in the ash tray. "What is it you say—ancora cigar?"

Giorgio shook his head and tried to grin. "No, grazie," he said. He stood up and took a deep breath. "It is all right if I . . . 'sleep on' the business of Pepi?"

Harry shot a surprised glance at Betty. "All right?" he repeated. "Of course it's all right. After all, we really have nothing to say about it. The whole thing is up to you."

"Up to you, up to you, up to you," throbbed the accordions and the violin from the beach.

Giorgio realized vaguely that Betty Clune, like Maria,

was a woman who could direct the traffic in a room without any apparent effort to do so. He found himself at the door, standing between them, Harry with his hand on the knob, Betty with the tips of her fingers lightly on his arm.

"You will think about it, won't you?" she pleaded.

"Si," said Giorgio. "I will think about it."

On the beach the riveters and assemblers and tuners of seaplanes threw the energy they had preserved during the day into a whirling, stamping dance against time, against the inevitable moment when the leader would fold his protesting accordion and reach for his bottle of grappa. Faster and faster, to hold back time. On the street side of the Hotel, Giorgio headed for the comparative darkness of the arcaded sidewalk across the avenue, moving slowly, breathing slowly, trying to think slowly. Slower and slower, to hold back time. And on the shelves of Friedrich Theus, the Swiss watchmaker, the clock faces stared dimly at one another from the shadows and prattled on, some dulcetly, some brazenly, but neither slower nor faster than always.

The watchmaker's shop was at the far end of the arcade from the Hotel. Jacopo, standing nearest its window, shaded his eyes and tried to peer inside.

"I wonder what time it is?" he said.

164

Benozzo consulted his smugly uncommunicative watch. "We should have had a signal," he grumbled. "The shade lowered. A cigarette thrown from the window."

"No one—" Carlo sighed—"throws cigarettes away these days."

Vittore said nothing. He was staring down the arcade, where the pattern of dark and light patches made by street lamp and columns was broken by a life-size figure in almost imperceptible motion.

"A sleepwalker," murmured Benozzo.

Vittore shook his head. "It's Giorgio," he said.

Jacopo's moonlike face became worried. "What's the matter with him?"

"He ate too much," declared Benozzo.

Vittore signaled for silence; they waited until Giorgio approached and gazed vacantly at them.

"A man with a face like this," suggested Vittore quietly, "bears bad news."

Jacopo nodded, biting his lip. Giorgio sighed heavily, and four sighs in unison answered him.

"Ah, well," said Benozzo, "it is as before. So we shall try again the next time."

Vittore reached up and put a comforting hand on Giorgio's shoulder. "Giorgio," he said soothingly, "a man must not feel sad when he has done his best. Of course," he added, "there is best and best. One man's

165

best is better than another man's best. It is possible that next time I should conduct the affair in person."

Giorgio recovered somewhat from his stupor and shook his head.

"You don't understand. The Americans *want* to adopt Pepi."

There was a stunned pause, and Jacopo's mouth dropped open. Then Giorgio nearly staggered under the impact of Benozzo's hand clapping him on the back.

"I told you!" Benozzo boomed jubilantly. "A wise one, this one! I told you he was only being cautious. Giorgio knew what he was doing all the time! And who told you so? Eh? That's what I want to know!"

Vittore seized Giorgio's limp hand and pumped it.

"Caro," he said proudly, "you played it like a game of cards! Even we, your best friends, could not see your hand!"

"It was magnificent!" Jacopo breathed.

Carlo, the practical, waved them aside. "What did they say?" he asked. "When will they take him?"

Giorgio shrugged and pulled uneasily at his ear.

"They want me to think about it," he said.

"Come," Benozzo ordered, rubbing his hands together. "We shall have some wine!"

Carlo looked at the others quizzically.

"What is there to think about?" he wanted to know.

"True," agreed Jacopo. "The thinking is over now."

"We'll have some wine," Benozzo said flatly. "If we must think, we'll think; if not, we'll not think. Wine is as good for not thinking as it is for thinking."

They would have started moving, but something in Vittore's manner made them wait while he looked closely at Giorgio.

"What is it, Giorgio?" he asked kindly. "What is this—'thinking'? What is going on in your mind?"

No, said Giorgio to himself. There will be all the same arguments all over again. Are *you* a rich man? Can *you* do for Pepi what rich Americans can? Can any one of us do these things? Have we not all agreed that Pepi should be adopted by Americans?

"Pepi is not unhappy with us," he said finally.

Carlo's face, if possible, lengthened. "A small boy knows nothing of happiness or unhappiness," he declared. "He knows only if he is hungry or if he is not hungry."

Giorgio bristled. "He is not hungry . . . except between mealtimes."

Vittore held up both his hands.

"Listen to me, Giorgio. A great author once wrote, 'One is never so happy or so unhappy as one thinks himself to be.' As it happens, the author was French. But it is a thought worthy of an Italian."

Giorgio turned away. "I don't understand things like that," he said.

"It means," Vittore explained patiently, "that Pepi only *thinks* he is happy."

"And do I only *think* I am unhappy?" Giorgio asked bluntly.

Vittore, for once taken aback, stroked the lapel of his coat.

Jacopo moved forward anxiously. "Are you unhappy, Giorgio?" he asked.

"We don't want you to be unhappy," Benozzo grumbled.

"But we must think of Pepi," Carlo reminded.

Jacopo untied the kerchief around his neck, but instead of mopping his face with it, he polished the end of his nose vigorously.

"I shall miss Pepi," he said in a curious muffled tone.

Vittore looked at him sharply.

"But I shall be glad," Jacopo continued quickly, "that he is rich and has such fine parents."

Benozzo, feeling a sudden small sting in his right eye, tugged smartly at his mustache and coughed. Still Vittore had not spoken, although Giorgio's eyes were on him expectantly.

"I am a thinking man," Vittore said finally, avoiding Giorgio's look. "A student of things. A man cannot study feelings if he also allows himself to feel them. According to logic, pragmatics and all superior con-

168

siderations, Pepi should go with the Americans. I await arguments."

There was none, since opposing Vittore in an argument was notoriously as foolhardy as leaving one's blinds open to the noonday heat.

"Good," said Vittore shortly, and he clapped his hands twice. "Pepi!"

Giorgio started. "Is he here?"

"We told him to wait," said Carlo lugubriously, "for the good news."

Giorgio shook his head. "We'll tell him tomorrow," he said.

Vittore sighed again.

"Giorgio," he said sympathetically, "the wine of today is drunk. Tomorrow we pull another cork and start fresh. Why should we save an empty bottle?"

Pepi sensed the importance of the occasion the very second he responded to Vittore's call. He planted his bare feet wide and waited eagerly, innocent of mischief and therefore deciding that the pervading gravity was only a joke.

Vittore took his hand soberly. "You are to be congratulated," he said. "You are going to be an American."

Pepi's grin faded slightly. He looked at Benozzo, looming over him with his mustache working.

"The American big shot," said Benozzo, "is going to take you to his palace."

"You will be rich," said Carlo.

"Very rich," said Jacopo.

Pepi looked up slowly at Giorgio, who cleared his throat and then nodded.

"It's true, Pepi. The Americans want you to go with them."

Pepi stared at him. "Do you . . . want me to go with them?" he asked.

Giorgio found that his hands, independent of his brain or the rest of his body, were waving foolishly in the air. He stopped them with an effort and thrust them into his pockets. Pepi immediately did the same. Benozzo blew his nose mightily.

Giorgio, failing twice to find his voice, bobbed his head up and down affirmatively, then turned and strode off into the darkness.

Inside the watchmaker's shop a clock began to strike, and then another, and another. And beyond the Hotel, on the beach, the music stopped.

Chapter twelve

Pepi

From the rooftop terrazza of Signor Veneto, the architect, the view of Finale Ligure was unparalleled. High on the fragrant, luxuriant hillside, it was a permanent reviewing stand overlooking a never-ending parade. A parade of colored sails dancing and dipping offshore, spangled umbrellas on the beach, automobiles blaring and chirruping at one another with truculent hoarseness as they threaded their way along the highway, and directly beneath the terrazza, peddlers, dogs, marketing women and bicycles maneuvering the steep, narrow streets of the upper town.

Signor Veneto enjoyed the superior feeling it gave him to anticipate the impending collision of two carts or the encounter of two old friends at a corner where neither knew the other was approaching. It was part of the pleasure accruing from the lifelong process of gaining altitude over his original five feet three. His studio, the room opening on the terrazza, was crammed with designs for towers and skyscrapers. That he was a builder of bathhouses reflected not the least on him, he would explain, but on the taste of the generation.

His observations on this score could be relied upon to enliven the morning coffee hour, usually shared by his close friend and neighbor, the olivegrower Giulio Bonelli, who would often leave his own breakfast table early for an additional cheering cup on the terrazza. Their friendship thrived, in fact, on this agreeable custom and on the fact that each could pursue a given topic of conversation without contradiction, or even acknowledgment, from the other.

"Take the new post office," said Signor Veneto. "Not that I am a vindictive man. Nothing could induce me to term it the monstrosity that it actually is."

"For a man to have only daughters," replied Signor Bonelli, "is a curious kind of joke."

"Even you," Signor Veneto insisted, "could never drag from me the admission that if *I* had been chosen to design it, they would at this moment be striking off a suitable medal."

"A single son," Signor Bonelli mused, "would reduce by one the number of young males one must regard with suspicion. First it is Giorgio. Then Ricardo. Then someone else and then Giorgio again. And now! Do you know who it is now?"

"A tower. Two towers perhaps, with roofs of copper. They would have been seen for ten chilometri."

"Ricardo. A man who makes airplanes and must take her riding on the handle bars of his bicycle. And Giorgio is no better. He hasn't even a bicycle. He *walks* to his cabana. And he has twelve years to pay on it."

Signor Veneto pricked up his ears. This was common ground.

"A very well-constructed cabana," he murmured modestly. "Although I would be the last to claim so, it will stand until it is paid for. Possibly even longer."

From their vantage point, Giorgio's cabana colony was a neat double row of cabinos and a gaily fluttering awning. A familiar figure darted across the highway as they watched, and a tiny Fiat squealed to a stop, five heads popping up instantly through its open roof and shouting imprecations.

"Besides," said Signor Bonelli, "what kind of husband for Maria is a man who runs across the Via Aurelia without looking!"

They both sighed and surveyed the unsuspecting town in silence.

Giorgio stopped beside his ice chest and looked in all directions. Not that Pepi wasn't perfectly safe somewhere. But where! He had not slept at home, or under a table at Benozzo's, or, according to Father Luigi, in the cathedral. Yet it was a warm night, he may even have fallen asleep on the beach. Early bathers had already helped themselves to some of the umbrellas and set them up on the beach; the invasion would surely have awakened a small boy. Giorgio blew his whistle and called.

"Hello," said a voice behind him.

He whirled in amazement. Pepi, sidling in from the highway behind him, was grimy from head to foot.

Giorgio looked at him reproachfully. "You slept in the goat yard!"

Pepi nodded. "Yes."

Giorgio took a deep breath and started automatically piling towels. "You wanted to be with your goat?"

Pepi shrugged.

"Well, what will the Americans think? Will they want such a dirty little rascal?"

Pepi grinned hopefully, and Giorgio swallowed several times; his throat was unaccountably dry.

"Go and get yourself clean," he ordered. "Go for a swim."

"I saw a shark this morning," Pepi announced.

"You did not."

"A big one."

"Go for a swim anyway. You'll scare him away."

"Will you come?"

"No," said Giorgio shortly. "I have an engagement for breakfast."

"Maria has a good head," said Signor Bonelli. "She could help him with his accounts."

"A well-constructed cabana," said Signor Veneto, "runs itself. People gravitate to it. People would come in the same way to a well-constructed post office. As things are, I predict that mailing will drop off in Finale."

In the Clunes' hotel room, Betty put down her coffee cup and bit into a peach thoughtfully. "Do you think he'll come?"

Harry nodded, blinking as he swallowed a scalding mouthful of coffee.

"I suppose you're right," she agreed. "He's so polite he'd probably come in any case."

Harry lighted a cigarette and put it out almost immediately.

"Are we doing the right thing?" he asked nervously.

She smiled. "Do you feel that way, too?"

"I don't know. It's hard to explain. I mean . . . the whole thing gives you such a funny feeling. He seems to be agreeable to the idea, and yet—he makes me feel as if we're trying to take something that doesn't belong to us."

"He loves the boy, Harry," she said simply.

"Yes. I guess he does."

"He loves him more than he realizes himself."

He avoided her eyes. "We could do a lot for the kid," he said.

They were silent, knowing each other's thoughts. Yes, they could do a lot for a boy like Pepi. Yet if the handsome young Giorgio refused, it would have to be the end. It had to be entirely up to Giorgio.

Harry put his coffee cup beside hers and took her hand. Neither of them moved until the rap came at the door.

Giorgio accepted a cup of coffee and stood awkwardly in the middle of the room, wondering if the contractions in his forehead were as noticeable as they felt. Nothing had been said but "Good morning."

Harry cleared his throat. "I guess you know what we're waiting to hear," he said.

Giorgio gestured inconclusively with his free hand. "He is very dirty," he said suddenly.

Betty's eyes widened. "What?"

"Very dirty," Giorgio repeated. "You should have seen him this morning. And a liar! A liar magnifico . . . that is, terrible. A terrible liar. Today a shark. Another day it was a wolf on the goat path." His expression was one of extreme embarrassment. "There are no wolves. Or sharks."

176

Harry chuckled. "That isn't serious, Mr. Cappelletti." He smiled.

The sun glinted on Betty's honey-colored hair as she shook her head in relief.

"That's where—parents can help," she said gently. "Sometimes children lie to . . . get attention. To get love, understanding from their parents."

"That's right," said Harry heartily. "You see, you're a busy man. You don't have time to . . . well, teach him things."

I taught him to swim, thought Giorgio. I taught him to count towels and to tell a piece of iron ore from a piece of slate. I showed him how to wade into the grotto under Caprazoppa at low tide and how to shout so that the walls shouted back and then whispered. I showed him how to tell one racing car from another, and I took him up to Signor Veneto's terrazza with Maria and taught him the streets of Finale—with Maria. With Maria.

"Once a parent explains about lying," said Betty, "once the child understands that it might make people distrust him someday . . ."

She looked at Harry pleadingly.

"We think," said Harry, who seemed to be having great difficulty with his throat, "that we can do a lot for the boy. However, ask us whatever you like."

Giorgio put his coffee cup down firmly.

"No," he said. "I will get Pepi cleaned up. Maybe," he suggested painfully, "you will take him for a ride."

Harry seized his hand, and Giorgio winced at the pressure. "You bet we will," he said gratefully. "Whatever you think best."

"It is best," said Giorgio dully. "Everybody says so."

"There he comes again," said Signor Bonelli. "He should spend more time at his business and not visiting at the Hotel."

"Artistically, the Hotel is a disgrace," Signor Veneto observed.

"After all, there is no one to watch the cabana but the little boy, Pepi. And he won't be here long, I hear. Some Americans are going to take him with them when they leave Finale."

"Everyone leaves Finale," said Signor Veneto dolefully. "It is architecturally uninspiring."

"That is one thing about having daughters. You hear all the gossip. Maria is usually as bad as any of them, but this morning she had nothing to say. I shall never understand daughters."

Pepi was seated on the steps leading down to the beach, his back against a stack of furled umbrellas. An empty soft-drink bottle stared challengingly at him from the sand, but he disdained it. One of his curls dropped over his eye, and he swept it away angrily. Even when

Giorgio sat heavily beside him on the step, he kept his eyes stubbornly on the horizon.

"What big lies have you got to tell me now?" asked Giorgio threateningly.

Pepi started, and turned in spite of his resolve. "Lies?" he asked.

Giorgio slapped his hands together fiercely.

"Yes, lies! Lies! You lie to me all the time, why not now? Go ahead—lie to me!"

Pepi swallowed and blinked.

"Have you seen no more sharks? No bandits? No pirates?"

Pepi shook his head.

"*Why?* Why do you always lie to me!"

"Because," said Pepi uncertainly, "it makes you laugh."

Giorgio frowned at him suspiciously, then looked away from Pepi's puzzled stare. "That is because I am a big fool. Lies are bad. Lies make people . . . distrust you. Don't you *know* that?"

I don't think I ever want to grow up, Pepi thought. I'll never understand the other grownups.

"I only tell very big lies," he said cautiously. "I won't lie any more, if you don't want me to."

Giorgio stood up and waved his arms. "It isn't me!" he shouted. "Why do you make it *me!* It's everybody. It's not something I made up."

Then, abruptly angry with himself, he sat down again.

179

"The Americans are coming to take you for a ride in their automobile."

"Yes, Giorgio."

"You are not to forget, the American is a big shot. A very important man. You must be polite, or they will change their minds."

"Yes, Giorgio."

A cough behind them made them both turn.

"Benozzo!" Giorgio gulped, unwilling to believe his eyes.

The mustache bristled with dignity. Benozzo smoothed his ancient bathing suit and planted his canvas-shod feet in what he supposed was a military stance.

"It is a good day for a swim," he rumbled defensively.

It was to be a morning of miracles. Five minutes later Carlo arrived, unrolled a pair of faded-blue swimming trunks from his apron and demanded a bathhouse.

Almost on his heels, panting with excitement, Jacopo trotted into view, brandishing canvas shorts.

"Is it permitted?" he asked, blushing slightly. "In my house there is a shortage of swimming suits for men."

Giorgio glowered at them, unable to share Pepi's unrestrained delight.

"I know," he said darkly. "You are the 'flanking army' again. You think I'm not to be trusted!"

Benozzo let his mouth fall open; his air was one of

childlike innocence. "Trusted, Giorgio?" he boomed.

"Vittore sent you!" Giorgio accused. "Not one of you has been in the water for ten years. You can't even swim! Jacopo—you even hate to take a bath!"

"That is true," Jacopo admitted. "But only because cleanliness is not good for the cheeses."

"Then if you're going swimming, why don't you go? Why do you stand there, watching me? I'll tell you why —because you know the Americans are coming and you are going to report everything I say to Vittore."

"Not at all," said Vittore himself mildly, strolling into their midst and leaning an inflated inner tube carefully against the ice chest. "It is a fine day for a swim. I should like to be assigned to a bathhouse, Giorgio."

But the millennial spectacle of Vittore in a swimming suit was not in the cards. For at that moment the blunt maroon nose of the Clunes' big car eased to the curb beside the cabana entrance. Pepi backed quickly behind the umbrellas.

Giorgio grimaced at his companions and controlled an impulse to hiss and flap his arms. Instead he smiled unhappily at Betty Clune.

"These are . . . my friends," he said.

Benozzo, sensing a flicker of amusement in Betty's quickly averted eyes, applied a restorative to his dignity by lighting a cigar. Vittore bowed, and for several minutes the heat of the day served its classic purpose

181

as a conversational stimulant. Present heat, potential heat, relative heat, historic heat and New York heat having taken their proper turns in both English and Italian, Vittore was, in fact, prepared (from having had some experience in meteorology) to discourse at length on cloud formations and convection, except that Pepi's curiosity began to overcome his reserve, so that a small brown face appeared between two of the gayest umbrellas. It was, Pepi decided, a very giant of an automobile.

"Would you like to ride in it?" asked Harry carefully.

Giorgio translated. One of Pepi's feet emerged tentatively.

"He's not sure of us." Betty smiled. "Does he know much about America?"

Giorgio shook his head.

"In America," said Harry slowly to Pepi, "you could have a dog."

Giorgio repeated in Italian.

"I have a goat," Pepi replied promptly.

"Er . . . he says he is very fond of animals."

"Try him on a baseball bat," suggested Harry.

Giorgio complied, and Benozzo obligingly pantomimed a bastone di baseball with his cigar.

Pepi hesitated, nodded without conviction and terminated the audience by retreating once more among the umbrellas.

"Maybe even a baseball uniform," Harry called. "Regular shoes with cleats."

Knowing Pepi's emphatic attitude toward shoes with or without cleats, Giorgio edited his translation. A muffled murmur came from the umbrellas.

"He's very rude," said Giorgio.

"Not really," said Betty warmly. "It's a little sudden for him, that's all."

Harry snapped his fingers. "I know what it is!" he said. "He doesn't understand we only want to take him for a ride. He thinks if he gets in the car, he won't ever come back." He turned to Giorgio. "Can you explain to him that he won't have to leave today? Maybe tomorrow, or even the next day."

Maybe tomorrow, then, there would be no lean, elusive form darting among the bathers and flashing along the water's edge in pursuit of an unwary gull. Maybe the next day there would be no sly hand dipping skillfully into the bottles of raspberry soda. Maybe the day after that there would be no solemn little companion at the top of the hill path to share the gift of the golden morning. The stones by the wall beside Father Luigi's chestnut saplings would be safe from scurrying feet, Fortunato's tempting lemons would joggle untouched in the rickety wagon. There would be on more wolves or sharks or pirate ships in Finale Ligure. There would be no Pepi.

183

"The schools are very good in the town where we live," Betty was saying.

Giorgio shook himself. He stole a sidelong glance at Vittore and Benozzo, who favored him with bleak stares.

"School," he said. "If Pepi hears us talking of school, he might run."

Ostensibly for Jacopo's benefit, he repeated the sentence in Italian.

"Yes," he said loudly a third time, again in Italian. "I am sure he would *run.*"

There was a scurrying of bare feet on the sandy boards, and the umbrellas quivered.

Giorgio sighed and avoided the eyes of his guests. "You see," he said helplessly. "Now I may not find him all day!"

Harry's automobile keys jingled as he shifted them from one hand to the other. Otherwise, to Giorgio's mild surprise, no one moved.

"I'll go after him," Giorgio offered guiltily. He began wishing someone else would speak.

It was Betty who said quietly, "I think we ought to let him come back of his own accord."

"If he does come back," Harry said, examining his keys as if he hadn't seen them before, "we'll be at the Hotel."

He shook hands all around and followed Betty to the car.

On the terrazza of Signor Veneto, Signor Bonelli was taking his leave.

"It is Wednesday," he said. "One of my daughters will come over later and sweep for you. Probably Maria. She is out of sorts today for some reason and refuses to work in the olive grove. But she needs to be occupied."

Signor Veneto protested, as always, and Signor Bonelli insisted, as always. Signor Veneto would take warning and be absent, since cleaning depressed him. But Wednesdays were Wednesdays, and this Wednesday was surely no different from any other Wednesday.

Chapter thirteen

No Pepi

THERE will be a battle, Giorgio thought. Carlo will scold, Benozzo will threaten, Jacopo will reproach. And Vittore will reason with deadly logic. And Maria. Maria will curl her lovely lip at weak, sentimental Giorgio, whirl on her proud heel and marry someone else. Probably Ricardo. But not Ricardo of the arrogant profile and the gleaming smile. Oh, no. For first Ricardo will meet Giorgio on the avenue and will have the bad grace to fling a scornful taunt. And Maria will marry Ricardo of the mashed nose and the loose teeth.

He doubled his fists and squared his shoulders. "Well?" he growled.

The four Ricardos reeled, receded and came into focus. One was slight and square and wore a coat. Another was large and chewed the end of a mammoth mustache. Another was round-faced and perspiring. And the fourth drooped like a garment supported by a single clothespin.

Benozzo removed the end of his mustache delicately from his mouth.

"She should not have mentioned school," he said.

"School is a good thing," said Carlo doubtfully.

"School," Benozzo announced, "is for scholars. And baseball bats are for baseball players."

"There can be no argument," said Jacopo.

Vittore fingered a red patch on his inner tube. "It was a very big automobile," he said in a tone of reluctant fairness. "Heavy and fat, of course. Not like Italian cars."

Giorgio stared at him, unbelieving. "It was a fine car!" he declared.

"The Alfa Romeo is a fine car," Vittore retorted calmly. "The Maserati is a fine car. There is surely no finer car than the Ferrari. I have had some experience with automobiles, the Bugatti in particular, and I have this to say. The Mille Miglia was won five times by——"

"Stop!" Giorgio roared. "Do *you* have any of these fine cars? Do *I?*"

Vittore shrugged.

"As for dogs," Jacopo ventured, "I do not care for them. They do not give milk."

Giorgio wheeled to face him.

"What are you trying to do!" he shouted. "You change my mind one way, now are you trying to change it the other? For days you tell me it is best for Pepi to go to America. All right it is *best!* It *is* best! Why did you let him run away and not try to catch him? Where will he live in the winter when I am working in the iron mine and he must go to school?"

Benozzo blew contemplatively on the lighted end of his cigar.

"There is a little room," he said, "under the eaves of my restaurant. I have kept wine bottles there. It is not a good place for wine bottles. It is not . . . a bad place for a boy."

"Why didn't *you* chase him, Giorgio?" asked Carlo reasonably.

Giorgio ignored him. "Where will his clothes come from? Can he wear wine bottles?"

Ex-corporal Jacopo Manzoni heard the faint sound of bugles and straightened bravely.

"My sister Angelina's uncle by marriage," he proclaimed, quickly crossing himself, "has no further need of his clothes. My sister Josefina could be persuaded to sew. She is very lazy, but chiefly about cooking."

"And money?" Giorgio challenged hoarsely. "Who has so much money that Pepi can buy books and pencils and rolls to eat?"

188

Vittore laid the inner tube aside carefully.

"We have considered this too, Giorgio," he said **matter**-of-factly.

Giorgio was able only to stare at him incredulously.

"It was a warm night," Benozzo reminded him. "Everyone was lying awake."

"As it happens," Vittore continued, "we have a certain amount of money we did not know we had."

Giorgio swept a pile of towels aside and steadied himself against the counter. Jacopo, he was informed, had decided to diet. Specifically in the matter of aperitivi; he had resolved henceforth to drink only two instead of three each evening. And Benozzo had reckoned in his usual orderly fashion that an appreciable profit could be achieved if he smoked somewhat fewer cigars than he sold. As for Carlo—well, there was a certain percentage of tips that might be saved.

"From Americans only," Carlo added hastily. "It seems a sort of justice."

"In addition," Vittore concluded, "there are a few books of which I have no further need."

"But—we agreed it was . . . best for Pepi . . ." Giorgio said shakily.

"Pepi," declared Vittore firmly, "is a very big liar. He runs away when he should not. He is sometimes dirty. And in the absence of proof to the contrary, it may be stated that he is not entirely innocent of stealing. Is this

189

any kind of boy to send to America as an example of young Italian manhood? No. He is our own burden. We must accept it."

Giorgio discovered that there was salt spray on his cheek, although no breeze was blowing.

"You are all very foolish," he said. "*I* made Pepi run away, not you. *I* have done all the things that have been done wrong. I will accept the room where the wine bottles were stored, and I will accept Angelina's uncle's clothes. But I will not accept the money."

"It is not for you to accept or reject," said Vittore sternly. "We are taking Pepi from you so you can be married."

"No!" Giorgio yelled. Then more quietly: "I mean no. No." He folded his arms forbiddingly across his chest. "No."

"But Maria——"

Giorgio slammed his fist on the counter. "Stop telling me what to do!" he cried. "I am a man, not a . . . a committee!"

He walked stiffly away from them and looked up and down the highway.

"The committee is adjourned," Vittore decided, "for the time being."

Giorgio blew a peremptory blast on his silver whistle. Its shrill reverberations blended into the morning chorus of Finale Ligure—the cries of flower sellers, children and policemen, automobile horns, dogs, somewhere a radio playing *Il Trovatore*—but there was no answering whistle.

Giorgio turned back into the cabana, his face openly perplexed. "He's really run away!"

Vittore pursed his lips and raised an eyebrow.

"The committee," he announced, "is in session again."

"Someone should tell the Americans," suggested Benozzo.

"It is a matter requiring a certain degree of diplomacy," said Vittore. "Perhaps it would be well if I——"

Giorgio interrupted with a wave of his fist. "*I* will tell the Americans," he said.

Betty, in a dark-blue traveling suit, opened the door. Harry looked up from fastening the last suitcase.

"Oh," he said. "We didn't expect to see you again, Mr. Cappelletti."

"I want to explain," said Giorgio.

"You don't need to." Betty smiled. "I think we understand."

She held out her hand, and he took it guiltily.

"We've been talking about it," said Harry, straightening from his task. "We think . . . well, you're a pretty fine man, Giorgio—may I call you Giorgio?"

Giorgio nodded.

"We don't blame Pepi for wanting to stay where he is. And we don't blame you for deciding to keep him."

"You knew I decided to keep him?" Giorgio's tone was puzzled.

"We knew it," Betty said softly, "before you did, Giorgio."

Giorgio felt his neck reddening. Then suddenly he felt almost at ease, aware of an indefinable atmosphere, something transcending the torn rug, the chipped and worn furniture so rudely exposed in the streaming rays of the sun. It was a setting bluntly ill-suited to deep feeling, yet Giorgio no longer felt his English inadequate or his manner awkward. There was an understanding in this room, and the fact that no one spoke for a moment was simply the exchange of a silent tribute.

Giorgio smiled. "Excuse me," he said. "Since I am going to keep Pepi, I think I had better find him."

For his share of the search, he had selected the section of town between the Piazza XXV Aprile and the Hotel, and extending from the beach front across the highway and up into the olive-green terraces. He started with the Hotel, asking Sergio, the cook, who swore by the eyes of Machiavelli that any little boy who might have invaded his kitchen so near the luncheon hour would have been skinned and chopped for a rabbit. Gino, the waiter, patiently pasting tattered lire together, com-

192

plained that the state of currency kept him too busy repairing tips to notice runaways.

Giorgio crossed the highway and tried the little shops in the arcade. Favorite haunts of Pepi's—the whispering, ticking clock shop, the caraway-scented bakery, the spaghetti factory with its rows of white, festooned drying racks.

"Pepi?" Friedrich Theus, the watchmaker, spoke in a gentle, meticulous purr like the voice of one of his own clocks. "I have not seen him, Giorgio."

Emilio, in the spaghetti factory, paused in the singing of the basso profundo role of *La Forza del Destino*, shook his head, and launched into a tenor aria from *I Pagliacci*. In the bakery, cassati especially reserved for a visit from Pepi were untouched.

It was the same everywhere. Ambruzzi, the fisherman, mending apparently the same places in the same nets, thought he might have seen a small boy in the Piazza Oberdan, but it may have been yesterday.

Fortunato, rounding a precarious corner in his wagon, stopped to sympathize.

"He cannot have run far, amico. No boy makes a serious business of running away without first stealing supplies from my wagon. And nothing has been stolen."

At the service station of Giusti Bergamo, a famous racing driver was signing autographs and posing for newspaper pictures. Overhearing Giorgio's question, the driver swept his retinue aside and volunteered his services.

"I have officiated at every kind of civic affair!" he exclaimed. "But never at a kidnaping. We shall pursue the criminals in my car. It will make a fine story!"

Giorgio politely rejected the offer and withdrew while the reporters frantically revised their captions. *The Famous Racing Driver Participates in a Search for an Abducted Boy!*

There was a puppet show in the Piazza Oberdan. But among the delighted children hugging their sides with laughter there was no Pepi.

A policeman fanning himself in the shade of a corner osteria and regarding the impossible tangle of local traffic with resigned tolerance lifted his helmet and scratched his head.

"Runaway boys seldom consult the police," he stated. "Our policy is, in fact, opposed to running away, but then our advice is rarely sought. Public servants," he confided, "are not appreciated."

He made a laborious entry in his book, and Giorgio climbed the crooked streets toward the upper town. In front of a tobacco shop he encountered the mayor, Signor Ghigliamo, in earnest discussion with Father Luigi over the protocol of a forthcoming Saint's Day.

"Lost?" echoed Signor Ghigliamo, removing a mutilated pencil from his teeth. "When I return to my office I shall order a proclamation!"

"Pepi can't read," said Giorgio respectfully.

Father Luigi demanded the whole story and listened carefully. "Since you practically *told* him to run away," he reasoned, "he must be hiding in some place where he knows you will look. In the grotto?"

"I don't think so. I've told him never to go alone and especially not at high tide."

"Then with a friend."

Giorgio appealed to the skies with both hands.

"Who are his friends? Benozzo. Carlo. Vittore. Jacopo. They are looking for him, too! Maybe he thought I meant for him to run *far* away . . . even away from Finale Ligure."

Father Luigi shook his head. "You will find him waiting for you in a place obvious to him and unlikely to you. And, Giorgio—I should like to talk to you about Pepi one of these days."

Giorgio hung his head. "I know," he said. "There is the matter of school."

"School," Father Luigi agreed, "and other training. Since you tell me you are going to keep Pepi, you have elected a serious responsibility. There are things from which neither you nor Pepi can hide."

"The authorities," intoned Signor Ghigliamo.

"The Authority," Father Luigi corrected, smiling.

There it was again. A small boy needed guidance. What could prevent him from running away whenever he saw fit? Who was there to see that he attended school and learned his catechism? How could an iron miner be in two places at once? And how could he explain to Father Luigi, especially in front of Signor Ghigliamo, that the only girl he would ever love had made him choose between Pepi and her?

"Excuse me," he said forlornly. "There is no use deciding anything about Pepi unless I can find him."

The next corner was a familiar one. From here the precipitous street to the right led straight to the Bonelli house. Or the equally steep alley to the left would take him near the summit of the ridge, where Signor Veneto's lofty studio and terrazza overlooked the town. From the terrazza, he decided, he could survey the whole of Finale Ligure and perhaps discover a hiding place he had missed. And Signor Veneto's door was always open. He toiled up the alley to the left.

Chapter fourteen

Finale Ultima

Vittore in the meantime had organized the
other divisions of the search at a table in Benozzo's. The
beach from the Hotel veranda down the entire length
of the town to the Sciusa river bed, now summer dry,
and beyond to the seaplane factory itself, was assigned
to Jacopo and Carlo, who covered their area with a
thoroughness born of opposite motives.

For Jacopo it was a highly exciting adventure. He was
a secret agent whose true identity would shake the idle
pleasure seekers to their bare soles if they could pene-
trate his disguise. He would pad stolidly between the
rows of umbrellas, whirl suddenly, bend down and con-
front a startled party of picnickers with a fierce stare.
Or he would march purposefully in one direction and

abruptly change his course, hoping to catch his prey off guard.

In the matter of overturned boats, which could be ideal hiding places, he was masterfully devious. After making a wide circle around the boat, he would yawn elaborately, stretch out on the sand for an apparently innocent nap and seek his potential quarry with deceptive, half-closed eyes. Once he even hesitated beside a sun bather whose face was covered suspiciously with a towel; there is no predicting where his zeal might have led him at that moment if Carlo hadn't dryly remarked on the unlikelihood of Pepi's masquerading as a fat man.

For himself, Carlo counted every step taken in the sand as equal to two on a solid surface. His own diligence, therefore, was inspired by a heartfelt desire not to have to retrace any steps. Relying largely on his skill at observing details, he would periodically adopt an advantageous position and peer in every direction while Jacopo went rolling away from him like a ball from a stick.

It was Carlo who thought of interviewing the cabana proprietors, all of whom knew Pepi by sight, and in this way generally spreading the alarm. Since the noon hour was near, the inevitable surge to the cabana verandas had begun, and by afternoon almost the whole of Finale would be on the lookout for the runaway.

Those who remained in their doorways or in the shade of the Spanish Arch were already being approached by Benozzo, who had gratefully changed from his venerable bathing suit and was exploring the central portion of town. Being Benozzo, he undertook his task with forthright mien, his mustache at so menacing a tilt that two of his old customers paid their delinquent bills without being asked.

The Piazza XXV Aprile and its tributary streets milling as they did with a wondrous vehicular and mercantile confusion, losses of one sort or another were far from unusual. Not only stores but cellars, stairways and balconies were scoured almost daily for anything from tourists' handkerchiefs to wayward donkeys who had slipped their rope harnesses. It was nothing for the townspeople to join enthusiastically in the search for a missing automobile (which usually turned out to have been parked in the Piazza Oberdan instead) or, on at least one notable occasion, for a missing cinema star (who turned up several hours later in the back row of the cinema).

In the present instance the cinema was one of the first places to look. Benozzo stole in the side door, waited until his eyes became accustomed to the dark and his ears to the characteristic clamor of the audience, recognized the film as American, concluded that the man in the story would be captured as usual by the girl, satisfied himself that Pepi was not there, went out by the front door and righteously demanded his money back.

Within an hour he had visited every commercial establishment in the neighborhood and had thrust his head into doorways, boxes, automobiles, buses and baskets alike. Only one place remained; he took a deep breath, filling his lungs with the protective fumes of his cigar, and strode into the corner restaurant of his Sicilian rival. This, he said to himself, hardening his senses against the mingled smells of fish, Marsala and Caciocavallo, is the ultimate sacrifice.

Angelo, the Sicilian, greeted him like a wealthy cousin, and it was not until after lengthy amenities that Benozzo was able to ask his question and retire, puffing frantically on his cigar.

"I suppose—" Angelo groaned inwardly—"that now I shall be forced to return the visit. Santa Maria, if I must enter Benozzo's restaurant, let me survive the smells!"

Dejected, Benozzo ducked his head under his own awning, looked sharply to see whether Tonio had cleaned away the glasses he must have broken, and stopped short at the sight of Vittore, who apparently had not moved from the table where he first planned the search.

"Where have *you* been looking?" Benozzo asked accusingly.

Vittore sighed patiently. "As you know," he said, "I am a man of logic. I *know* where Pepi is."

Benozzo spluttered indignantly.

"Then why have we been turning the town upside down this way! If you knew——"

"I did not say I *knew* where Pepi was," Vittore corrected. "I said I *know*. By simple elimination, it is a fact that he is not in this neighborhood, or you would have found him. By the same process, it becomes a fact that he is not on the beach, or Carlo and Jacopo would have found him. He is not at the west end of the town, because a small boy running away does not run toward his own home, which is in this case Giorgio's. Therefore, having estimated the places Giorgio must have looked already, I know where Pepi must be."

"Then why don't we go and find him?"

"Unless I have made a mistake in my calculations," said Vittore, shaking his head, "which I'm sure you will agree is a minor risk, I don't believe it will be necessary. I will go so far as to say that something significant may come of this!"

A town on the sea, more than most towns, may be said to have a face. It turns its best side unquestionably toward the sea, so that an observer standing at the stone railing of Signor Veneto's terrazza has a feeling of being behind Finale Ligure as well as above it, and therefore a sense of watching without the town's knowledge.

For some time the watcher had been Maria Bonelli, elbow on the scoured railing, chin in hand, dampened broom forgotten and drying idly in a corner. The view, for all its familiarity, was an ever-exciting one and often drew her from her Wednesday cleaning of the architect's studio.

To the east and west there were the two immense promontories jutting out into the golden Gulf, with the long, honey-yellow town between them. Far to the right, past the top of the Arch, the Basilica, the roofs of the square shore-front buildings, past the last of the cabanas and the seaplane factory, a yawning gap in the sheer rock of Caprazoppa swallowed one continuous stream of automobiles and emitted another. In the other direction, over the flat-topped houses of the Varigotti section, the pennoned casteletto on the lofty top of Crena Point displayed its battlements like rows of even teeth. Closer, between the Hotel and the center of town, vehicles and pedestrians eddied perpetually, the highway traffic struggling to disengage itself from local affairs.

For once, however, Maria noticed all of this only briefly. Her large, thoughtful eyes had scarcely left the figure of one man as she followed his erratic course up through the streets and alleys. He had been only a distant form at first—easy to pick out, of course, from his springy athlete's gait—and from the occasional glint of the sun on the silver whistle that jounced on his chest. But now, at the last turn where he had paused a moment in indecision, he was life-size, running his unmistakable fingers through hair that could be no one else's. She could have sworn she could see, rather than only sense, the inevitable wrinkling of his brow.

Now he had made his decision and was threading his way through the last and nearest alley, so steep that narrow steps served for a pavement. He climbed over a preoccupied artist on the top step and charged into the entrance three floors beneath her. And he was on the stairs, bounding noisily two steps at a time and probably swinging himself around the corners by bracing a hand against the wall. Maria loosened the yellow kerchief that had held her hair and let the blue-black cascade tumble around her shoulders. When Giorgio stamped through the studio and stopped in the doorway, she was busily sweeping the bricks of the terrazza.

"Maria!" he exclaimed.

She flourished the broom dramatically. "Giorgio!" she mocked, her eyes impenetrable as always.

"Wh-what are you doing here?" he stammered.

"*I* am here by permission," she said coolly. "Because men are unable to do the simplest things for themselves, even when it comes to knowing one end of a broom from the other. And you? What are *you* doing here?"

"I came up here to look for Pepi," he said foolishly, and because she accepted this with a toss of her head as if it were the most natural thing in the world, he felt more stupid than ever. "That is . . . I don't mean I expect to find him *here*."

He jumped aside as her broom briskly threatened his feet.

"If I were looking for someone," she remarked, continuing to sweep vigorously, "I should look in places I did expect to find him. But of course you're a man. Men have brains so huge they must make everything more difficult."

With a look intended to convey offended dignity, he walked around her and leaned on the parapet. There was a small boy pushing a bicycle up the hill, and there was another curled in a doorway diverting the course of a patient beetle with a stick. Another, trudging along an alley with a long loaf of fresh baker's bread, stopped to put his loaf on the cobblestones and scratch his back against the wall. The figure sunning itself in presumed privacy on a roof near by was very obviously not a small boy. Giorgio turned away in embarrassment and was startled to discover Maria looking at him covertly.

"Pepi is hiding," he explained. "He ran away."

The broom swished furiously over a spot already swept four times.

"In that case—" swish—"you'd better hurry and find him—" swish—"before the Americans change their minds." *Swish. Swish!*

Hypnotized by the motion of the broom and the even more disconcerting undulations of the sweeper, Giorgio stared until he felt his face begin to twitch. With a single sudden stride he wrested the broom from her and threw it into a corner.

"The Americans don't have to change their minds," he shouted. "I have changed my mind and sent them away. They can't have Pepi! *Nobody* can have Pepi!"

For some reason he could not possibly explain, he wanted to shake her. He had an overwhelming urge to reach out to where she stood, feet widespread, hands arrogantly on her hips, and seize her by the shoulders. He wanted to shake her until she cried for mercy. He knew it was a silly, meaningless impulse, another piece of nonsense in the goat's brain someone had substituted for his own. Consequently, he was even more surprised than Maria when he found himself carrying out the urge.

He shook her until one of her earrings fell off and then stopped abruptly, waiting for a breathless tirade that never came.

"Next time," said Maria calmly, brushing the hair out of her eyes, "tell me you're going to do that, so I can put my earrings in my mouth."

"Nobody can have Pepi," he repeated. "He belongs to me."

He retrieved the earring and handed it to her. "And if you won't marry me *with* Pepi, you . . . you can't marry me at all!"

He turned, plunged through Signor Veneto's studio, knocking a limestone paperweight to the floor and descended the stairs two at a time, bracing himself against the wall as he took the turns. He lurched blindly down the steep alley, nearly collided with an organ-grinder at the corner, aimed a kick at a can of refuse and painfully injured his toe, and limped angrily on a zigzag course to Benozzo's restaurant.

Benozzo shaded his eyes with one hand, perceived that it was indeed Giorgio approaching, and called within. "It's Giorgio! He's found Pepi!"

This is the silliest of all, thought Giorgio, as Jacopo tumbled eagerly out of the restaurant, followed more sedately by Carlo and Vittore.

"I haven't found Pepi!" he contradicted, leaning over to rub his throbbing foot.

Benozzo grunted and turned to the others for advice. Not being a man to distrust his own senses, he accepted as palpable fact precisely what everyone else in the vicinity accepted, and that was the undeniable spectacle of Giorgio stumping across the square, black as a thundercloud, followed at a respectable distance by Pepi, who had, in fact, been following him almost the entire distance.

Pepi himself now settled the question by walking the remaining distance to where Giorgio stood. "You told me to run away," he reminded.

Giorgio gulped. "Where did you come from?" he demanded.

"Signor Veneto's," said Pepi. "I was hiding there. Why are you so angry with Maria?"

"You heard all that?"

"Of course. You were very funny. I almost laughed aloud, but I didn't because Maria told me to be quiet when she hid me."

"*Maria* hid you!"

"Naturally," said Pepi. "I went to her house first, but she said she was going to Signor Veneto's. We both laughed after you had gone, of course."

Giorgio appealed to the others with both hands, then turned back to Pepi. "Why in the world did you go to Maria's house?"

"Because," said Pepi simply, "I knew if you should change your mind, she wouldn't let them take me."

Giorgio clapped the heels of his hands in distress.

"Benozzo!" he moaned. "Vittore! Listen to this, all of you! It is a good thing I have decided to keep Pepi—he needs me badly. When he thinks he is in trouble he goes straight to his worst enemy!"

"Maria is not my enemy!" said Pepi in surprise.

"The important thing," Benozzo interrupted, "is that the affair is over. I have been saving for an occasion like this three bottles of Lambrusco."

Jacopo sighed heavily, and even Carlo straightened and rubbed his hands.

"Lambrusco," said Vittore judiciously, "should be drunk on a hillside in the sun. With peaches. However," he continued quickly, "it would be impolite to refuse. The first bottle will doubtless create the hillside and the second the peaches."

Giorgio took Pepi firmly by the arm.

"Didn't you say she laughed at me?" he demanded.

"Yes." Pepi nodded. "We both did. Perhaps we weren't laughing at *you* exactly. I think we were laughing because we were happy."

"The Lambrusco——" Benozzo began.

"Giorgio has something else to do," said Vittore. "Maybe he will join us later."

"I have something to do," said Giorgio. "Pepi, go and take care of the cabana."

He looked resolutely at Vittore, who stroked his cheek and nodded.

"I think," said Giorgio matter-of-factly, "that I may be crazy."

He turned slowly and walked along the north side of the Square toward the upper town.

"He has stopped limping," marveled Benozzo. "You see what even the *mention* of Lambrusco can do!"

Giorgio found Maria after turning only two corners. She was wearing a red-silk blouse and white skirt and was sitting on a stone bench beside the street under a palmetto. He thought she was the most beautiful thing he had ever seen.

"What are you doing?" he asked.

"Waiting for someone."

He sat down stiffly. "If you want to marry me *with* Pepi," he said, "of course you can."

"Thank you," she said.

"I am probably a big fool," he said, a little loudly because a ringing in his ears interfered with his hearing.

She nodded and carefully smoothed her skirt. "You are the biggest fool in Finale Ligure," she agreed.

The ringing stopped and there was a sudden heaviness in his chest.

"Ricardo?" he asked with great difficulty.

"Ricardo?" she repeated. "There is Ricardo, my third

cousin in Padua. There is Ricardo the winegrower, Ricardo who works in the bank, Ricardo, my ten-year-old nephew——"

"Ricardo the foreman at the seaplane factory!" he said hoarsely.

Her eyes widened innocently. "Is his name Ricardo?" she asked.

Giorgio bit his lip. "You're making fun of me."

She stood up and stepped very close to him, her eyes blazing.

"Don't you think you deserve it?" she accused. "I said you were the biggest fool in Finale Ligure! Don't you want to know *why?* Because you never even knew that if you had let the Americans take Pepi, I should never have spoken to you again in all my life!"

He was stunned. "But . . . you said . . . you told me——"

"I told you to make up your own mind, and I told you I wouldn't marry you until you *did* make up your mind!" Suddenly her voice was very soft, and for the first time he could ever remember, he could look deep into her eyes. What he saw made him inexpressibly giddy. "Do you think I could love a man who had so little love in him that he would let strangers take away his little boy? Pepi is yours, Giorgio. Now he will be mine, too. That is—if you would like to ask me properly to marry you."

210

In that winged instant the new Giorgio thought of a thousand gilded phrases. The eloquence of centuries flowed through his brain in a poetic torrent. He selected at random from a blazing firmament of words.

"I love you," he said.

The next night two empty bottles stood on the table at Benozzo's, and from the third Lambrusco foamed rosily into five somewhat unsteady glasses. Pepi, curled on a chair in the corner, kept his eyes open with difficulty and against orders.

"I told you to go to sleep," Giorgio said sternly.

"Yes, Giorgio," said Pepi, closing his eyes and immediately opening one of them again.

"He is a good boy," said Benozzo for the fifth time. "He will have fine Italian parents as he should."

"It was what you wanted, eh, Pepi?" Carlo smiled.

Pepi nodded, entranced by the first real smile he had ever seen on Carlo's face.

It had been a day of smiles—and of wonders. One of those magical days when things had seemed to go right for everyone. For Fortunato, who was so remarkably pleased with the world in general that he broke a lifetime rule against little boys on his wagon and swung Pepi to the high, rickety seat for a proud ride through the streets of the Neri section. And for Emilio, so happy that he beckoned to Pepi from the door of the spaghetti factory, generously shared his lunch and gave a private performance of the entire score of *La Sonnambula.*

It was something in the air, Pepi had decided. Both Carlo and Jacopo had insisted upon sharing their lunches as well, and Carlo had demonstrated his darkest and most thrilling secret, a heart-stopping trick of making the Hotel elevator grind jerkily to the sixth floor and slip terrifyingly to the fifth. Vittore had allowed himself to be relieved of a pocketful of sweets, and Benozzo let him copy an entire menu on the blackboard in his slow, round lettering.

Everyone seemed to want to give something away, too. Ambruzzi, the fisherman, who saved odd bits of cork, pressed upon Pepi the prize of his collection, an absolutely round cork float with a mysterious rattle inside. Signor Veneto, meeting Pepi in front of the Casa Municipale, drew from his pocket an extraordinary limestone paperweight and thrust it at him with the off-hand explanation that it had suffered a tiny chip and was of no further use to him. And queerest of all, Ricardo, pedaling to lunch from the seaplane factory, had squealed to a stop and presented him with an airplane carved from a single piece of beech.

Giorgio had sniffed slightly at the airplane, but then Giorgio had apparently spent the entire day in another world and was not accountable. Ordinarily, for instance,

212

he would have taken Pepi to task for neglecting his duties at the cabana, but today all rules were somehow forgotten. And anyway, Maria, who for some reason had found the cabana particularly inviting, winked at him and promised to see that no towels were stolen.

He could not have explained why the sight of Giorgio and Maria, mooning at each other over the ice chest, made him wriggle with delight. It had something to do with the fact that Maria's eyes were different and that there were no wrinkles in Giorgio's forehead. Or maybe it was that he felt his own sudden contentment had spilled over and gone right to the people he wanted most to share it with. Whatever the reason, it had been a memorable day, full of friendly things and laughter.

There was still laughter now, as the five glasses clinked again and again in Benozzo's restaurant and as Carlo rose a bit uncertainly to his feet.

"Since this is the last glass," Pepi heard him say, "I think there should be a toast."

Through heavy-lidded eyes, Pepi saw them all look to Vittore, who stood up in turn.

"I agree," said Vittore. "But since the last toast should always be made by the oldest or the youngest, let it be made tonight by the youngest of us, who today has become the oldest."

It didn't make any sense, thought Pepi sleepily, but from their shouts they all seemed to understand. With his last waking glimpse, he saw Giorgio stand, grinning a little foolishly at first, and then becoming very serious.

"I am not a scholar like you, Vittore," Giorgio said slowly, turning his glass in his hand, "or a man of the world like you, Benozzo. Or a philosopher, Carlo. Or a man with rich friends in New York, Jacopo."

"That's four toasts!" Benozzo exclaimed.

"Maybe." Giorgio smiled. "Or maybe it's five. Because I want to drink to something that Father Luigi told me, but that I had to learn for myself. He said, 'The heart is often right.' "

Pepi, slipping into unconsciousness, was aware of a silence.

"That's my toast," said Giorgio, and the glasses clinked once more.

"He's asleep," Jacopo whispered, nodding toward Pepi.

"It's been a fine evening," said Vittore. "An evening on a hillside, with sunshine and peaches and good companions."

Giorgio gathered Pepi's limp form into his arms and nodded a good night. Twenty minutes later he stood at the path by his house and turned back. There was no moon, and the stars seemed to vault right from the sea to the mountain behind him. He shifted the small burden on his shoulder and looked at the town, where only the street lights and one fisherman's lantern gleamed an

214

answer to the stars. He could see the dim, stately outline of the Basilica against the faintly shimmering sea, and as he watched, one light flickered on in a back window far down on the Via Aurelia; Giuseppe the baker was getting up to light his ovens.

He felt, rather than saw, the great, comforting bulk of Caprazoppa on his right, and his own breathing seemed to be the breathing of the mountains and the Gulf and the sleeping town. His last glance was across the upper town where the house of Giulio Bonelli the olivegrower hid in the warm darkness. Then he looked down at Pepi and turned again toward his own house.

"My grandfather also said," he murmured to the sleeping boy, "that the truest thoughts of all are those that come at the end of the day."